A MULTITUDE OF SINS

Zoe Morgan is now a part-time marriage guidance counsellor, a far cry from her exciting days as a police officer working with Cloughton CID. When one of her clients seeks advice, Zoe assumes she is embittered after years of unhappy marriage. A week later Graham Crowther is killed attempting a dangerous canoeing trick at his local club. The club coach is not convinced Graham would have attempted such a stunt, especially alone, and Zoe draws on her old detective skills to look into the increasingly suspicious death. Did Linda Crowther opt for a more violent way out of her marriage...?

A MULTITUDE OF SINS

For my sons-in-law,
Ian Domville and Jamie Barker.

With my thanks to and great respect for
Lis Horrocks-Taylor, who shared her
experiences with me.

A MULTITUDE OF SINS

by
Pauline Bell

Magna Large Print Books
Long Preston, North Yorkshire,
England.

British Library Cataloguing in Publication Data.

Bell, Pauline
    A multitude of sins.

    A catalogue record for this book is
    available from the British Library

    ISBN 0-7505-1174-5

First published in Great Britain by Macmillan, an imprint
of Macmillan Publishers Ltd, 1997

Copyright © 1997 by Pauline Bell

Cover illustration © Last Resort Picture Library

Published in Large Print 1997 by arrangement with Macmillan
Publishers Limited

Magna Large Print is an imprint of
Library Magna Books Ltd.
Printed and bound in Great Britain by
T.J. International Ltd., Cornwall, PL28 8RW.

Chapter One

Linda Crowther sat on a bench in the town precinct and stared at the shop window display in front of her. Huge wreaths of plastic imitation fir were entwined with strings of tiny lights that flickered on and off. The wreaths were linked by loops of scarlet velvet ribbon, tied at each extremity of the window in huge bows. Linda appreciated the designer's talent but felt no surge of Christmas cheer.

It was only the second week in November, for goodness' sake, and the shops were already so full of Christmas tat that there was nothing worth taking. That didn't really apply to Marks and Spencer's, she supposed. The good basics were there as usual, but the garments were partified and the table decorations festively seasonal, not suitable for general use. And then there was the stepping-up of security to go with it all, though the extra crowds compensated, made her feel safer.

She concentrated on the left-hand window with its white satin pyjamas and the black lace nightdress with tiny ribbon straps. It was elegant but not for her.

7

Graham would tear those straps the first time he pulled it off, though it would be from general ineptitude and clumsiness rather than uncontrollable passion. Thank goodness for small mercies.

That was rather an elegant white sweater over the other side of the window. She got up and went nearer to examine it. Yes, it appealed to her. She decided to investigate exactly where its clones were displayed inside. There was a whole rack of them, rather too near the door for her purposes, but she could always pick one up and wander further inside with it. She fingered the soft angora and admired the design of the beading round the neck and cuffs. Then she sighed.

Close-fitting sweaters were difficult. Jackets were easier. You could pop them on without using the aggressively supervised changing rooms. She could hardly slip into a clingy evening jumper out on the shop floor. Unfortunately, she had already acquired more jackets than she knew what to do with. Never mind, she would change her plan, pick up some underwear and some pretty knick-knacks for Helena. She'd choose a size too big. That way they would be sure to fit her eventually. Better than getting something too small, since she wouldn't be able to change it without a receipt.

Linda wondered whether it was worth the risk. Helena was a lumpy and unattractive child however she was dressed, but one had to make an effort. It was a pity she couldn't bring her to try things on, see if there was anything that might improve her, but you could only shop with a child in tow if you intended to pay.

Well, she'd get Helena sorted out here. Later, she'd get herself an evening sweater from Molloy's.

As a preliminary to her afternoon's efforts it would be necessary to buy some small thing. Then she would have an uncreased plastic carrier bag, obviously newly acquired for her legally obtained purchase. She felt in her pocket to assure herself that the minute pair of sharp nail scissors were at the ready for the removal of tags. She hoped the C&A method of weighting garments with locked-on security discs would never gain favour in here.

M&S had become very security-conscious lately. There was only one way to steal with the advent of security cameras: be very up-front. Accost the salesgirl. Ask for another colour or size. Ask to be accompanied to the door to see the colour in daylight, preferably when the assistant was too busy and said she was sure she could trust you. Parade around in your prospective 'purchase', viewing it from all angles, having rammed your own garments into the top of your shopping trolley. The trolley hardly projected the image she was anxious to acquire but it was a necessary evil. Chat to another customer meanwhile. 'I'll have to go and ask my daughter, over there with the pushchair'. Walk up to the security guard at the door and chat to him. 'Still raining, is it? Oh, well, back on with my mac.' Stand right beside him as you drape your raincoat over your purloined garment and ask him if he doesn't find it hard to concentrate all day just on watching people.

It was a pity her eventual objective was to be found out. To begin with, it had been her primary goal, but she had discovered that she had quite a talent for thieving. It gave her a kick for its own sake and it had vastly improved her wardrobe. In fact, she'd had to produce a convenient mythical 'seconds' shop, near the university, that she supposedly patronized when she visited Peter, to account for her new smartness.

She collected a selection of frilly knickers and a couple of bright winter dresses, labelled 'Age 4-5', removing the tags the sales staff would normally retain. Then she deliberately tripped and dropped all the packets in front of another customer. She held open her bright green carrier-bag and allowed the old lady to cram the purloined items into it, thanking her profusely and berating her own clumsiness. Still chatting to her, she walked at the old lady's pace to the door. That would do for M&S. Now for her sweater.

The best place would be Cloughton's one remaining old-fashioned department store. She made her way to it in the part of the town left high and dry when the new arcade and the new bus station were built a few years ago. It didn't matter. The people who shopped at Molloy's remained loyal.

Security was still lax here. The customers who came in had their wallets or their bank accounts full. No need to put their reputations on the line to get what they wanted or relieve their resentments by pulling a fast one on a successful family business. They were more likely to identify with it.

There were official rules about how many garments could be taken into a changing cubicle but Linda knew that no close watch was kept. It was easy to take in one, even two, extra. Then you brought out the proper number and occasionally bought one of them. It was important not to come here too often. Molloy's customers were not impulse buyers, not always popping in looking for bargains. They were secure in the knowledge that when they actually required something

11

there would be plenty of money to buy it, and, if exactly what they had in mind was not available, they had the clout to get it made so. They were no 'snappers-up of unconsidered trifles'.

She resented them, but their way of life meant that pickings here were still good. It was a pity that their choice of apparel and therefore the stock that the shop carried, though of excellent quality, was somewhat dowdy and staid, the colours muted and 'classic'.

She had set her heart on a beaded jumper and she couldn't bear to disappoint herself. She ascended two floors to women's fashions. She must choose carefully. The labels here spoke for themselves. She mustn't strain the credulity of her friends about what she could afford to pay even if her clothes were supposed to be slightly damaged seconds. She looked at the expensive evening wear but, perversely, preferred the cheaper M&S version to these stiff and elaborate designs. There was no point in taking something she wouldn't wear. She was tempted by some of the glamorous underwear but she didn't succumb. She had enough trouble with Graham as it was. She wasn't going to encourage him.

Then she found it: a silky, sleeveless, round-necked blouse comprising less than half a yard of fabric but beautifully cut, tucked and embroidered. It cost £45. She was thrilled with it on all counts. It suited her purposes in every way. She edged into a corner and removed the filmy scrap from its hanger. She made no secret of her admiration of it, holding it up and scrutinizing the delicate stitching. Then she slipped it on to another hanger, underneath a hideous, long-sleeved satin creation. She took that and one of the beaded velvets into the changing cubicle, letting the salesgirl carry them and hand them in to her.

She tried on the skimpy blouse and admired her reflection for a few seconds before taking it off. It was small enough to be screwed up and pushed into her pocket. She grinned to herself and put on the satin shirt. It was a hard electric blue that lent her cheeks a purplish tinge and emphasized the fading of her hair. She drew back the curtain and displayed herself to the salesgirl, smiling ruefully. 'I must be losing my touch. I can't think why I thought it would suit me.' She returned the two garments to the girl and reclaimed her trolley.

The heat of Molloy's had been suffocating. Linda stood in the street, drawing in great lungfuls of cool, drizzle-dampened, diesel-scented air as she fingered the smooth silky fabric crammed into her pocket. The creases would soon fall out when she put the blouse on a hanger. She would begrudge the £45 she had omitted to pay if they didn't!

Chapter Two

Frank Carr sighed with relief as the singer on the platform indicated that his last encore had been his final one. He wriggled in his unyielding seat to relieve his cramped buttocks and politely joined in the storm of applause with as much feigned enthusiasm as he could muster.

His concert ticket had been bought by his flu-stricken girl-friend and he had humoured her by attending so as not to waste it. He was reminded of his mother, insisting that he finish food that he neither needed nor enjoyed, for the same reason. He decided that his attending the concert had done as much good to Zoe as his overeating had done to the starving African children.

At least he had swelled by one more the large audience this renowned singer would certainly have expected. He wondered what this celebrity, accustomed to the great concert halls of the capitals of Europe, had made of the decorations—and of the acoustics—of Cloughton's 'Vic'. It had been built in the heyday of the monarch so flippantly referred to and exhibited all the extravagant excesses of the period, from flocked wallpaper to monstrous lightshades which the music and drama critic of the local paper, Frank remembered, had irreverently likened to glass versions of Ali Baba's turban.

He clapped a little harder as he remembered that it was only a few minutes' walk from the concert hall to the Crossed Keys, where a tap on the bar supplied what the regulars called Falling Down cider. His spirits rising, Frank moved with the rest of the departing audience out of the plum-coloured velvet stalls into the gloomy corridor that led to the foyer.

Here, all was glass and glitter, from chandeliers and huge gilt-framed mirrors set into the wall panels. In one of them, he caught sight of an acquaintance. Rob Cameron was instantly recognizable, even as part of a milling throng reflected in a slightly distorted Victorian mirror. He stood half a head taller than most of the men present, the head further distinguished by impressive dreadlocks. His attire, too, marked him out, the singing yellow of his immaculate sports shirt mocking the black ties and lounge suits.

Frank pushed through the departing crowd until he could catch Cameron's attention by touching his elbow. 'I've been hoping to run into you, Rob, to ask

16

if you've thought any more about getting another dog? The bitch I was telling you about whelped last night. Most of the litter is spoken for already but there's a good little female still up for grabs.'

Cameron indicated in mime that, in the pub, they would be able both to slake their thirst and hear each other speak. Ten minutes later, their tankards contained as modest an amount of 'Falling Down' as would allow them to remain on their feet, and Frank's evening began to brighten.

The two men drank contentedly, discussing first the aforementioned animal's pedigree; then the concert, which Cameron had enjoyed; and finally, the affairs of the local canoe club of which both men were members. Frank was an enthusiastic new convert to the sport. 'Zoe wants to have a go. I knew she would.' His tone implied disapproval of his girl-friend's intentions.

Cameron brushed it aside. 'Why ever not? Bring her along. Seeing that she's your other half, I'll personally give her the full works.'

Frank grinned. 'I'm not sure I like the sound of that.' His expression became serious. 'I appreciate the offer though...'

He was interrupted by a commotion in the doorway that drew the eyes of most of the drinkers. The singer, Laurent Gilbert, whose performance of German

17

lieder—he supposed all lieder had to be German—had left Frank so unimpressed had been brought in to join his thirsty audience. Soon, with glass in hand, he was proving to be very good company.

Looking up, Cameron gave a small exclamation. 'It seems we're not the only musical canoeists in Cloughton.' Frank's eyes followed Cameron's gesture. 'Graham Crowther, at the great man's elbow—as you'd expect. See the glazed look in the poor man's eyes.'

But Frank thought the singer looked remarkably interested in what Crowther had to tell him. He had half turned away from the main group and had not shaken off the hand Crowther had laid on his arm. Frank was curious. He indicated Cameron's glass. 'More Falling Down? I reckon two grown men can manage another half.'

He approached the bar by a circuitous route that took him within earshot of an unusually animated Crowther, and hoped that his weaving was not being attributed to his cider consumption. He had put his reputation on the line for nothing, however: Crowther's exciting tale was ended. 'All that was before Linda came on the scene and I became a model husband,' he finished coyly.

As he returned to his corner after a

lengthy wait at the bar, Frank noticed that now the singer's eyes really had glazed over. Instead of working himself back into his place on the bench he suggested to Cameron that they make a rescue bid. 'We can't let Graham bore him to death. Such a loss to the concert platform!'

Cameron reached for his cider with a resigned shrug. 'Fair enough, though I reckon Graham's one of life's victims, rather than a killer.'

It would be just a little more than a fortnight before his prediction was justified.

A little after midnight, Laurent Gilbert sank thankfully into the blissfully comfortable chair in his otherwise merely adequate hotel room. His audience and his hosts for the evening had been very hospitable, but, long before last orders were called, he had wanted nothing but a bath and bed. They had no conception of the strain of being the sole performer at an evening recital, particularly as he had been supported by the Cloughton Chamber Choir's talented but unprofessional and unfamiliar accompanist.

He was tempted to stay on here for a while, but he had rehearsal commitments in London, and waiting there for him was Jennifer, who made life elsewhere impossible for him to contemplate. It

19

had been interesting to spend a couple of days in her birthplace, exploring it for himself. It seemed an unlikely one to have produced her. Now there was just her dear old aunt to visit before he could leave. She had been in the audience tonight, but she had been surrounded by friends who had borne her off before he could approach.

Laurent exercised his aching neck, pleased that he had concealed his weariness from his fiancée's friends, if they still *were* her friends when she could meet them so infrequently. Now that Jennifer's international career was beginning to take off, maybe she would see even him only in passing as they each concert-hopped around the world.

He realized, with a smile to himself at this peculiar compound verb, that he was thinking in English, that he almost considered himself an Englishman. He stood up and pulled back the curtain. The sodium lights and the few still brightly outlined windows gave little clue to his surroundings, but his imagination provided the rather dismal greens and greys he had seen when he had moved into his room the previous day.

Late October did not always show England at its best. He loved the cool spring with its primroses and bluebells that represented the muted delicacy of the natural world here. Even in full summer, the wild flowers hid the grass, giving just a suggestion of colour. He much preferred it to the lush brilliance of the fields of sunflowers at home.

He had even learned to enjoy English winters, and, last year, had been delighted to be snowed up in his country house outside Leeds. His mother, on a visit at the time, had been horrified. Snow and Yorkshire pudding had sent her scurrying back to Bordeaux. Freezing drizzle and enchanting, tentative summers were a suitable setting for the phlegmatic, stoic English. He hadn't really become like them, but he loved them for companions. Now, on his periodic returns to France, the excited, gesticulating gabble of his relatives exhausted and irritated him.

He opened the window and let the cold gusts help to sober him up. English beer was hard to take when you'd been raised on the weaker French kind. He'd still had his wits about him, though, as he'd listened to the ramblings of a certain Mr Crowther, and he'd been well rewarded for his polite attention. Suddenly, the information he'd wanted for so long had been presented to him, unsolicited and unexpected.

He scrapped his plan to return to London

by train the following afternoon. He would
hire a car and drive back. That would
give him time alone to decide what
to do.

Chapter Three

It was mid-November. Friday afternoon. Raining. Zoe Morgan, recovered from her flu, made a conscientious effort to offer her last clients of the week the same degree of attentive concern that she had given the others, but she was tired, and later, when she needed to, she would find it difficult to recall the exact turn of phrase, the precise tone of voice.

The lithe walk as Linda Crowther entered her office led Zoe to estimate her age in the late twenties. Proximity, however, revealed fine facial lines, the tint that masked a few grey hairs and, when the flaps of expensive soft black leather were unbuttoned, a small amount of spare flesh which had settled, as it does in middle age, where it thickened the waist and padded the stomach.

Mrs Crowther was perhaps a little unusual among her clients in that she was quite sure about what she had come for. 'I need to get rid of my husband. What I'd like you to do is to help me to screw myself up to it.' That explained why she had come alone.

It was not a task that Zoe had been set before. Not many of her clients were so direct. She wondered whether Relate's new premises had depressed Mrs Crowther and if these new surroundings would dispose others to give up on their partnerships before any discussion of them had even begun. This disused Victorian Methodist church was a warren of a building (apart from the huge central cavity in which its members had actually conducted their worship). The first test for Zoe's clients—or maybe the second, after their stint on the waiting-list was getting themselves to her office along depressing, echoing corridors, with paint peeling from their walls.

The office itself, too large for intimacy, had last been used for evening classes. The sink in the corner had its plumbing on display, the chairs were uncomfortable, a desk and filing cabinet its only other furniture. And Zoe could see that, whatever Mrs Crowther had expected in the way of a counsellor, it was not herself.

Nevertheless, a series of six hour-long sessions was agreed on and Mrs Crowther needed little encouragement to begin her confidences. 'I've come on my doctor's advice. Presumably he thinks all my symptoms are psychosomatic. That's because I told him that if I didn't have to cope with Graham, I'd have a bit of time to spare for looking after myself. By strange GP's logic, he decided I should come here to get my marriage patched up.'

Zoe smiled. 'We don't patch up. We explore options.'

'I know that. It's easier to be flippant.' She took a deep breath to continue her recital.

Less than half-way through this first contracted hour, Zoe began half seriously to fear for the woman's life. Not that she was suicidal—in fact, in her own way, she was manifestly enjoying herself. The danger seemed rather to be that her husband might snap, criticized beyond endurance. Nevertheless, Zoe let the catalogue of his shortcomings continue. Whether or not it was justified, it would be necessary to allow the woman to free her torrent of pent-up grievance as a preliminary to considering constructive suggestions.

With the session in its last quarter, however, Zoe was beginning to feel that Mrs Crowther's resentment had not been pent at all, that this glib soul-baring was well rehearsed, had been delivered to many a hearer before herself. Maybe it had been written and revised in years of diary-keeping, to become this articulate, orderly, recital. Or perhaps the long-suffering GP, having learned the script by heart himself,

25

had decided to prescribe a new audience for his patient.

In Zoe's opinion, it was probably Mr Crowther who needed counselling, if he was determined to go on living with this wife. She was curious about him. The appointment had been made for both partners. Where was he? 'The two of you obviously changed your minds about coming along together.'

Linda Crowther frowned, put out by the interruption. 'He only decided at the last minute not to come. Let me down as always.'

Let her down, Zoe supposed, by not being present to witness his humiliation. There didn't seem to be anything else she needed him for. Certainly not for his opinion of her pronouncements. After a few seconds' silence, Zoe began again. 'I'm assuming you don't have children?'

'Why?' Fair question, Zoe supposed. Why had she? Wouldn't most mothers have mentioned them by now? 'We've two, as a matter of fact. Peter's in his second year at Keele and Helena is three and a half. She's a Down's child.'

Was this what had soured her? 'Did your problems with your marriage begin with the shock when Helena was born, or even, maybe, when she was conceived such a long time after your son?'

'They began when my husband and I met.'

So why had she married him? Still, they'd consider that later. 'Does either of you blame the other—for the genetic accident?'

Mrs Crowther remained silent but shook her head. Zoe waited. 'He's impatient with Helena, and jealous of her, of the attention she gets. He'd like her put away, thinks it would give her a better chance, more intensive treatment.'

'Has he said that's what he wants?'

'He doesn't *say* anything.'

'Anything at all or anything about Helena?'

'He just won't talk. He says I'm clever with words and I always win so he just clams up. It makes me powerless. He won't listen, either.'

Who could blame him? She wished the husband had come, if only to be shown it was possible to shut his wife up. When Linda Crowther continued, her tone was ironical. 'He makes his views known in other ways. He considers himself a man of great principle—wears a CND badge, refuses to buy goods produced by countries with oppressive regimes—but it's all negative, an attempt to define himself, to borrow what others stand for.'

'What work does he do?'

27

'Building-society clerk.' The tone was contemptuous.

'Interesting work?'

'No.' Zoe waited. 'He does the accounts that can't be programmed into computers, maternity grants and pay, part-months for leavers and new starters, temporary promotions and so on.'

'He'll need to be meticulous.'

'But not enterprising.' A further silence, before she began again. 'It's like being married to a clockwork toy. You wind it up, face it in the right direction—'

'The right direction for whom?'

She ignored the interruption. '—and let it go till the mechanism you've set up runs down.' Zoe thought this was a fair description of how Mrs Crowther was conducting their interview. 'Then you do it again, bolstering him, encouraging him, just to keep him jogging on, ticking over. I can't relax. I'm afraid of what would become of him.' He might settle down, Zoe supposed, and enjoy some peace.

'Is he grateful to you?'

'Sometimes.' She heaved a deep sigh. 'It leaves no time for my plans for myself, though. I love it on the rare occasions when the firm sends him away on a course. It leaves me free to try to be myself. I couldn't just leave him, live with the idea of him floundering without me. I wish he'd

28

run off with somebody.' Her expression changed. The idea was obviously new to her and temporarily the rehearsed recital was abandoned. 'I wouldn't mind if he had an affair. If someone else liked him enough to want him it would make me respect him a bit, but no one does, of course. I'll only be free when he's dead. Are you shocked?'

Zoe shook her head. 'I was just wondering what it is you want to do with your life that your husband's getting in the way of.'

'I've never had a chance to think about it. I just know it isn't what I'm doing now.' Zoe glanced at her watch and Mrs Crowther began to gather up her outer wrappings.

Zoe motioned to her to remain seated. 'Is it possible to get someone to mind Helena for a day?'

'I suppose so, if it's a one-off.'

'Then, before we talk again, I suggest you plan and carry out a whole day's activities that don't involve your husband. You said he got in the way of plans you made for yourself. Choose one of them and follow it up.'

'My mother would take the child but I don't think that Graham—'

'Try him. I look forward to hearing about it.'

Zoe opened all the windows before she could face writing up her notes. Glancing down at the car-park as she straightened the curtain, she watched her client tip-tapping along in her elegant Italian leather shoes. At least, she reflected, the husband's despised building-society employment enabled his wife to dress like royalty when she came to complain about him.

The following Thursday evening had been chosen for Zoe's first canoeing lesson. To allay the slight nervousness which she refused to acknowledge and to while away the time as she waited for Frank, she reached for the local paper.

The *Cloughton Clarion* was half-way through a series of Thursday interviews with the various members of the town council. Tonight its front page was emblazoned with a colour picture of Leon Glasby, though it was not his turn for the spotlight. It was Zoe's opinion that he had bargained to be last on the list, so as to eclipse all the others.

In the meantime, he contrived to have a feature about one or other of his exploits alongside each of the reports on his colleagues. Today, he was pushing a state-of-the-art wheelchair, occupied by a decorative young female, up a newly constructed ramp, the result of his personal campaigning, according to the caption. It led to the almost as new 'leisure complex' in the town centre.

Zoe wondered which unthinking architect had designed it without a ramp in the first place, and how much of the interior of the complex was still inaccessible to the girl whom Leon was delivering, with such self-congratulation, on to the pad which activated the automatic door.

She looked harder at the photograph. That was an expensive electronic chair. The only reason she could find for Leon to be pushing it was so that he could receive the coyly grateful simper of the paraplegic girl. Zoe read more of the text, knowing it would anger her. Leon was much quoted. 'These people have an even greater need to be able to use the leisure-centre facilities than the rest of us.' Perhaps a girl who simpered like that did not mind being one of 'these people', smugly set apart from 'the rest of us'.

She was surprised at the animosity she felt towards Leon. It was a dozen years since she had seen him except at a distance, and even at school, where she had seen him every day, it had been only on the periphery of her vision. The only thing they had had in common was the ability to command their pick of partners of the opposite sex from amongst their sixth-form peers. He had been an extraordinarily good-looking youth, but she had disliked him and never accepted his favours.

He was still handsome, in a raffish sort of way, but he was not wearing well. After a further perusal of his features, she decided spitefully that good works did not suit them.

As the article took up most of the lower half of the page, Zoe almost missed a small paragraph of greater interest to her. 'A verdict of "death by misadventure" was passed today on Mr Graham Crowther, whose drowned body was found on Sunday below the weir at Crossley Bridge. He leaves a wife, Linda, a son, Peter (19), at Keele University, and a daughter, Helena (3). Funeral arrangements are to be announced...'

Zoe forgave the *Clarion* the understandable prominence it gave to the showman councillor and awarded it a star for sensitive journalism. No melodrama about the drowning and no mention of the little girl's disability. She read the short paragraph through again. Could Linda Crowther have possibly...? 'To get rid of my husband' had been an odd expression to use. It had been early on in the interview and, at the time, Zoe had assumed that Mrs Crowther merely lacked the courage to walk out on him, or knew too little of the legal procedure needed to divorce him. She had felt that the melodramatic phrase had been deliberately used to emphasize her client's desperation.

Zoe dug out the rest of the week's papers from behind a cushion. Usually, she read them carefully and kept herself abreast of local events. As she had suspected, the details of the drowning were in Monday night's edition, flanked by another photograph of Leon Glasby, this time surrounded by the members of a Methodist church youth club. Monday was choir-practice night, when Zoe had time only to scan the headlines.

The report was full of surprises. Graham Crowther too had been a member of the Cloughton Canoe Club. She couldn't remember Frank's ever mentioning him. Aged forty-four, his very active canoeing was behind him but he had apparently done sterling coaching work with the younger members. Recently, the club had entered for their region's rodeo event in early December. Mr Crowther had allowed himself to be persuaded to make up their team and had met his death whilst practising pirouetting, a spectacular and risky manoeuvre that he had not attempted for some years.

Even making allowances for the recently dead having inevitably been totally faultless and full of charity to all men, Mr Crowther's efforts seemed praiseworthy. It was strange that his wife had made no mention of them. They hardly fitted into her picture of an unenterprising, negative personality, barely able to function in his mundane situation in a small building society.

When she saw Mrs Crowther tomorrow, she would ask—but would she see her? The woman had merely wished her husband out of the way. Having had her wish granted, maybe she was more likely to be out booking a world cruise to celebrate than seeking further advice. Though, judging by the way she had talked on Friday, she might come along this week to complain about Graham's lack of consideration for her in relinquishing his life at this particular time or in this particular way.

Unless...? No, women of many words were seldom women of action. For this one, talking probably had the same effect as the blood-letting practised by surgeons in the last century. It left her weaker, and more comfortable, but less capable of actually doing anything. Still, Zoe had told her client to carry out a plan of her own. The idea was absurd, but it stayed in the back of her mind, teasing her.

She wondered whether to hide the papers away again. This evening she was to embark on her own adventures on the river. Her keenness to begin canoeing was undiminished but Frank, reading about a death in the local river, might try to talk her out of her plans. After a minute she tossed the papers on to an armchair, realizing her foolishness in thinking that Frank would be ignorant of the canoeing accident. He was a club member. It was possible that he had been keeping the news from her so as not to put her off.

She glanced at her watch. His surgery would just be finishing so he would not be here for at least another ten minutes. She checked the simmering casserole in the oven, then switched on Radio 3. A full orchestra burst into the room, wildly energetic, all its sections playing repeated loud chords. Presently, only the brass continued them, much muted, whilst the strings took over above them until the piece finished.

The music was succeeded by audience clapping. Playing the game her church-organist father had taught her when she was a child, she frantically debated with herself. Identify the piece before the presenter announces it! There had not been enough bars by which to judge and the announcer broke in, smugly triumphant. Schubert's Great C major. Ruefully, Zoe awarded herself nought out of ten. And she had thought she was totally familiar with her favourite Schubert!

Apparently, the snippet she had caught had been part of the musical illustrations from a talk on the symphony, which was now to be played in full. Zoe preferred to hear symphonies at concerts. A big work demanded a big occasion to give due respect to its pattern of introduction, development and resolution. She switched the radio off and was glad to see Frank's car draw up outside.

He smiled at her through the window as he came up the path. Good. The surgery animals must all have been successfully attended to. Their owners and Frank had gone home happy. No dogs had been put down, no one told that the cat's only resort was pain-killers.

Zoe knew as soon as he entered the room that he was going to ask her again tonight. The signs were small but significant, the chief one negative: he had omitted to stop off in the kitchen and peer through the glass door of the oven to see what she was cooking for him. It was a shock. She'd thought their trip to the river would leave no time tonight for the soul-searching and argument that inevitably followed his proposals of marriage.

Hastily, she pushed Monday's *Clarion* towards him. 'This is a tragedy, isn't it?

Did you know him?'

'Yes. A little, anyway.' Frank pushed the paper away and kissed her with rather more concentration than usual at this time of day.

She had to keep him distracted. 'I'm sorry for him and his family and the club, but it hasn't put me off. I shouldn't think I'll get to doing pirouettes, whatever they are, for a month or two yet and...'

He switched on the lamps and regarded her gravely until she stuttered into silence. 'I gather, from your efforts to distract me, that if I persist you'll refuse me again.' She nodded. He sat in the armchair opposite her and was silent for almost a minute before asking, 'What if you knew that this was to be the last time I asked?'

Zoe too allowed some time to pass before she shook her head. 'I can't marry you at the moment, Frank, even if you don't ask me again.'

He leaned back in the chair. 'When might you reconsider?'

There was the ghost of the old, the very old, grin. 'When I can shoot the rapids without you worrying about it.'

Realizing the significance of the answer, he abandoned his attempts to persuade her and his serious tone. 'You'd better get to your first session promptly then. What's for supper?'

In an abortive attempt to dissipate the tension between them, they replaced their customary and companionable mealtime silence with industrious efforts at conversation. She was glad the food was at least nourishing, since they took little pleasure from tasting it. Whilst she poured coffee, Frank took up the newspaper again.

He contemplated the picture of Councillor Glasby, then raised an eyebrow as he accepted his cup. 'A young man known to do charitable deeds, not always by stealth.'

Zoe sniffed. 'Not even usually. Tell me about the canoeist. Did you know him?'

Frank considered. 'I suppose at least as well as I knew any of the others. He was an odd chap but I got on well enough with him. He helped me, and a lot of others, very patiently with the basics so that Rob Cameron could concentrate on the sort of specialist stuff he's trained for.'

'I'm surprised a small club like Cloughton's has a pro for a coach.'

'We don't, officially. There was a rumour...' He hesitated, but having begun what was obviously a remark detrimental to Cameron's reputation, he would do better to complete it than to leave Zoe to speculate. 'Four or five years ago, Rob was principally a runner who promised to reach international standard, but I've heard talk of a drugs offence at county level. Anyway, for that reason or another, he stopped running competitively, widened his horizons and went into coaching watersports. He grew up just down the valley before going off to Loughborough to do his sports science. By joining lots of little local clubs and groups he'd become quite an all-round sportsman by then. He's doing his bit now to keep some activities going for the next generation.' Zoe had begun to stack their dishes but Frank knew better than to offer help.

'Why did you say he was odd? Crowther, I mean.'

Frank got up and went to the window. At least closing the curtains against the chilly November evening was still allowed. 'He had a bit of a reputation for fairy-tales. He wasn't as well-off as most of the rest so he tended not to join in the social activities much. And his wife's not very keen on coming down and making contact with us. I've heard that's because they've got a small daughter who's handicapped in some way. He kept his end up with tales of his glorious past in an amazingly wide range of fields. They all treated him as a bit of a joke and now they feel terribly guilty for calling his bluff.'

Zoe's voice rose over splashings from the kitchen. 'You mean they meant to expose his lack of canoeing experience by challenging him to enter for this competition, and he took them on, then killed himself in the attempt?'

Frank shrugged. 'Looks like it. It's a pity you're beginning in an atmosphere like this. In some ways it might be better if—'

Zoe shot through the doorway, furious. 'You think my canoeing's a stupid idea, don't you?'

'No.'

'Yes you do! I can feel you bristling with disapproval.'

'No you can't.'

'But you'd be happier if I gave up the idea?'

Frank walked over to the magazine rack and stowed the paper tidily away. 'I suppose I'd be easier in my mind if you didn't do it—less anxious, if you like—but not happier. You are who you are. You need to face this challenge. That's the person I care about and I don't want you to be different. I admit I'll be glad when you're safely back on the bank.'

Without answering, she returned to the kitchen. Frank sighed as she closed the door behind her to shut him out. Then he crossed the room, absent-mindedly smoothing the carpet pile with his shoe and obliterating her wheelchair tracks.

Chapter Four

As willing hands pushed the wheelchair to the edge of the riverbank, it came into conflict with a sizeable clump of watermint. Zoe savoured the clean, piercing peppermint scent of its crushed leaves, admiring the way pairs of them grew up the hairy stems, and the handsome clusters of late flowers. They were still flourishing in this unusually mild November, in variegated greys which in daylight, she knew, would be lilac blue.

The floodlights were similarly washing out the colours of the plastic boats and the garish cagoules of the canoeists. The latter were launching their craft: climbing in, at risk, it seemed to Zoe, of life and limb, and demonstrating to each other their considerable competence. She failed to spot Frank amongst them. He had announced that he would follow his own usual procedure and leave her entirely in Rob's hands. Zoe was unsure whether he was tactfully trying to behave as she would wish, or sulking. Maybe he had decided that, if she wanted to drown herself, he was not prepared to be part of the audience.

Fear of drowning was not among the sensations she was presently suffering. She was a competent swimmer, albeit in a clumsy fashion. She could let the water take her useless legs and she knew her powerful arms would take her the short distance to the bank. If she became stuck in the cockpit, there were plenty of rescuers available. She was not even afraid of looking foolish in front of them. After the humiliations suffered in hospital—where she had spent considerable periods of time completely naked as other people changed her bedclothes, organized her bowel management, her catheter drill, dressings, turnings, physiotherapy and examinations—she was inured to physical indignities on her own account.

She was afraid, though, of disgracing Frank with her clumsiness, of damaging the club's expensive equipment, of possibly putting the members to inconvenience, even in danger, by her ineptitude. And she was awed, not so much by being in charge of a canoe as by the whole new life of physical challenge that it began and represented.

Rob Cameron began his spiel and she prepared to turn her attention to practical matters. 'You'll learn more in this first twenty minutes than in all the rest of your paddling career.' Zoe doubted this but went on listening. 'In canoeing, the learner does all the work, though my fellow-instructors would not thank me for saying so. You needn't worry tonight about doing everything properly, or about capsizing. Quite simply, if you make no sudden movements, you won't fall in.'

Zoe grew impatient. Frank had told her this already. She held her tongue, however, as Rob offered her an armful of paddles. 'Choose your weapon.' Only colour seemed to differentiate them and she made her choice. First they were to do a dry run through the paddling process.

'Hands on the top of the shaft, thumbs underneath, shoulder width apart...' A full thirty seconds of verbal instructions for one little movement! Zoe obediently rotated the paddle to achieve an imaginary stroke on the left. Rob took a deep breath for his next command. Zoe forestalled him.

'Now you reverse the movement.'

'That's right.' He looked half impressed, half crestfallen.

Zoe was amused, understanding how the knack of a physical manoeuvre was difficult to explain. When she had repeated the strokes several times to Rob's satisfaction, she was pleased with herself. 'It's like operating the throttle of a motor bike, isn't it?'

He looked surprised. 'I suppose it is. Is

that how you had your accident, coming off a bike?'

'No, off a balcony.'

'Want to tell me about it?'

Did she? She wasn't sure. 'Not in detail. I was a police constable, taken along on a drugs raid. One of the men we were after went out there to throw the stuff out before we found it. I went after him so he tipped me over as well.'

'Tough.'

'Coming off a bike would have been tougher. I was on duty. The Criminal Injuries people provided treatment, equipment and a generous pension.'

'So what are you doing now?'

Zoe shrugged. 'It's taken me two years to get where I am now. I'm not sure where next—except that it won't be what the police have offered me, sitting at a switchboard all day, intercepting calls that send other coppers out on exciting jobs. Meanwhile, for something useful to do, I'm putting in quite a lot of time at Relate.'

'Isn't that the fancy new name for the old marriage guidance people?' She nodded. 'I didn't know you were married.'

'I'm not.'

Picking up the warning-off signals, he scrambled to his feet, pointing to her kayak. 'One good rule of thumb with

44

boats is that the sharp end is the front and the blunt end the rear, so you're flummoxed when you find a kayak has both ends sharp.'

After a short struggle, he and a volunteer henchman had her afloat in the craft. 'There are several correct techniques for getting in, but I'll give you another rule of thumb that we all follow. "Scrabble in as best you can, preferably without getting wet".'

Zoe watched Cameron's arm muscles slide beneath the skin as he passed her her paddle. He appeared to be of mixed race, a fine physical specimen, honey-skinned with black curly hair, and seemed to have inherited all the most advantageous characteristics of whatever races had produced him. On the whole, Zoe liked him, but she was beginning to find his facetiousness tiresome. It occurred to her that it was his way of dealing with the embarrassment as his wholeness contrasted with her limitations, and she was disappointed. He was qualified to instruct people with physical problems and he should be able to cope with this aspect of the job.

She had been resigned to being placed in the boat tonight, but was determined to plot and practise all possible ways of attempting to launch herself. It was a calm evening and, on this stretch of the river, the water was as flat as river water ever is, but such movement as there was was encouraging the light craft to circle around. Zoe decided she was no more helpless than any other novice and turned calmly to Cameron for instructions.

He grinned at her. 'We'll start with the sweep stroke, a deliberate turn, since that's what the boat wants to do anyway.'

Following his instructions, Zoe executed a wobbly sweep stroke, followed by several slightly less wobbly ones. She used the power in her shoulders to compensate for the useless lower trunk muscles.

Cameron was impressed. 'Now, to get more power and control, push gently with your foot on the same side of the paddle stroke.' He drew in his breath sharply. 'I'm sorry, I...'

Zoe sighed impatiently. 'Just let the one apology suffice for the evening.' She applied herself once more to the paddle, circling triumphantly. Surveying her critically, Cameron suggested, 'This stroke is most efficient when your paddle is stationary in the water and the kayak moves. If you sweep too vigorously, the paddle will move through the water and you'll lose power.' Zoe took heed and improved her effort, satisfied by his return to a tone of command.

They worked hard together for a further twenty minutes, after which Zoe was delighted to be sent to join the other near-beginners who were getting used to their new milieu by rafting and playing games with a water-soaked sponge ball.

Before letting her loose on the water, Cameron had talked her through a capsize. Towards the end of the session, she had acquired sufficient confidence to demand to do it deliberately. She tested the depth of the water with her paddle and mentally rehearsed the rest of her instructions. Cameron could not forbear from prompting.

'Keep your hand on the paddle and lean to one side till you overbalance. Now, hold your breath and relax your legs—oh, sorry.' In her euphoria, Zoe forgave him his further *faux pas*. Leaving her kayak upturned so that the trapped air kept it afloat, she struck out for the bank. 'I can only swim with my arms, so someone else will have to grab the boat.' As willing hands rescued it and hauled her from the water, Zoe realized she was very cold. Back in her wheelchair, she headed swiftly for the changing rooms before Frank should notice.

As she put on dry clothes there, and afterwards as the club members put away their gear, she was aware that the atmosphere had changed, had become subdued. The talk was of Graham Crowther's death and the good service he had given the club. Zoe realized that the carnival atmosphere on the water had been brittle and that the shouted laughter of the young canoeists was not their custom. It was their statement, perhaps, that the sport itself was not to blame for their fellow-member's death, and that they were in a situation where they did not know the correct procedure.

With dawning horror, she saw that Cameron's awkwardness, too, could have been caused by his need to fulfil his obligation to her and conduct the coaching normally in the face of the loss of his friend. She had fallen into the worst danger for the disabled, that of self-absorption, of seeing things only as they might relate to her situation, when it was really quite irrelevant.

Half an hour later, as they all gathered round the open fire in the riverside pub, Frank was glad to see that Zoe looked warmer and less pinched. She was holding court to the club members and had obviously been a surprise to them. He had told them that she was twenty-nine, a year younger than himself, and that she was paraplegic. It had been

48

a travesty of a picture of her. He should have described her exuberance, her refusal to take the world seriously. He should have told them that her long blond hair had been shaved off when she had her accident, but that she had immediately grown it again, despite its now being difficult for her to manage.

During those long months of hospital visiting, Frank had been prepared to work hard at restoring Zoe's self-image, at convincing her that he at least still found her beautiful. But his effort was needless. He quickly realized that she was still in love with life, still vain, still confident of her power over the opposite sex.

There had been an initial period of shock and depression, of course, when it was unclear what degree of disability she was facing, but once her condition had stabilized and she had grasped the extent of the changes she must make, she had quickly begun to plan positively. Had returned to normal, in fact.

Or so it had seemed to Frank, until she had broken their engagement. They must begin again, she had announced. Frank must reconsider. She was no longer the prospective wife to whom he had originally offered himself. She was impervious to argument. Most of the ones he tried were greeted with contempt, or, worse, a bitter conviction that his pronouncements merely proved her right.

She was exactly the same person he had proposed to three years ago.

She was the best judge of that.

He had already reconsidered.

He had needed to reconsider? Didn't that prove her point?

He had reconsidered only at her insistence. In the new circumstances he still wanted to take care of her, help to make up for what had happened to her.

Frank sighed now at his crass stupidity. What had caused him to present exactly the protestations that would most infuriate her? Hurt at her rejection? Frustration at her refusal to listen to reason? He buried his nose in his glass as he watched her talking animatedly. He had known that she would settle easily into the group and identify with its aims and interests.

He was puzzled now by her extraordinary interest in all aspects of Graham's death. It was out of character for her to demand gory details. It was politely and sensitively done, but she had asked a host of questions and obtained information that was new to him too. He had not realized how much pressure had been put on Graham to make up the rodeo team. Nor had he previously heard about the fisherman who had been seen early on Sunday morning approaching the stretch of river where the body had been found. He had thought Zoe's attempts to pump him on the subject at home had been just her method of distracting him from his eighth proposal of marriage, but it seemed that she had really wanted to know what Graham had been like and what exactly had happened to him.

Frank realized it was his turn to buy a round. Fishing a note from his wallet, he handed it to Zoe. 'Off you go, slave!' He was amused by the corporate surprise caused by this departure from his usual impeccable manners and grinned round at his companions. 'Watch,' he instructed.

Miraculously, a way through the crowd of drinkers opened up for the wheelchair. When Zoe reached the customers queuing three-deep at the bar, her order was shouted good-naturedly to the nearest barman. Filled glasses were passed to her on a tray balanced on her knees and, in less than three minutes, she was back by the fire. They all roared with laughter. Frank did not quite understand why this trivial but blatant exploitation of her disability amused Zoe, when she impatiently scorned most compensatory privileges she was offered.

When the party broke up, well after eleven, he could see that she was flushed and euphoric, the combined effect of physical achievement, social success and a moderate amount of alcohol. She even agreed to let him drive her home, once it had been established that the reason was her mild inebriation and not weariness.

Relations between them were easy again and he was able to tease her as she made excited plans for further exploits on the water. She let him make the coffee and, when he carried it through to the sitting room, the voice of Tina Turner issued from the CD player. He nodded his appreciation of the concession. 'I can't understand why you don't like her. You respond to naked energy in other singers.'

She shrugged. 'I don't think she'll grow on me. You can take her back with you when you go.' So, he was not to be allowed to stay. He drained his cup with cheerful resignation.

Zoe removed Frank's disc from the player as he retrieved his jacket and keys. Maybe his addiction to raunchy rock singers was another quite serious reason for not marrying him. When she thought about it, it was not this one's naked energy she objected to, but her naked emotion, screamed out into many of her songs so that the melody was lost and sometimes the rhythm too. She communicated her feelings very successfully, so Zoe had to admit that

52

she practised an art form of some kind, but she considered it a disservice to music.

Her eyes followed Frank's back lights as he drove through the gateway and disappeared down the road and she felt bereft.

Only in bed at night did she realize the full impact of not being able to walk. Her chair could roll away, she could be taken ill, the house might catch fire, be broken into. There was the telephone, of course, but it didn't command an immediate response. She could not yet separate her desire to have Frank in her bed as her lover from her wish for his presence as her protector. Until she could he must stay out of it.

She closed the door and circled the room restlessly. Ms Turner had unsettled her. She would listen to something more soothing. Greek folk songs fitted the bill. Her father had taken her, years ago, to a concert given by Nana Mouskouri. At eleven years old, Zoe had been singing for several years in her father's church choir and was critical: 'She breaks all the rules. She begins just anywhere and slides on to the right note from there.' Nevertheless, the music had enchanted her. Since the concert, Zoe had never been able to dissociate the Mouskouri voice from the physical form, the fragility, the bright dark eyes and long dark hair, the shy manner.

She knew now that the lady was anything but shy, but her public image was less threatening than Tina Turner's, even in a recording. She had discovered, too, that the vocal technique was deliberate, not careless. The sound was vibrant, each song catching a mood.

Zoe sat still, giving her full attention to her favourite on this disc, 'Plaisir d'Amour'. She thought it one of the simple, elemental tunes, like 'Greensleeves', plucked out from the beginning of time.

When the song finished, she began her preparations for bed and the music was distorted by the faint whirring of the electrically operated hoist that carried her, suspended, between chair and shower and shower and bed. She was ready before the recital was over and sat amongst the pillows, listening to the final song. The high notes lingered, held up in the air, shimmering, almost visible. Zoe thought she would give up the use of her arms as well as her legs rather than be deaf and be deprived of this pleasure.

As the music finished and the machine clicked itself off, she gave in and allowed herself to sleep with the light on.

She woke earlier than usual on Friday, to a morning of powerless but cosmetic

November sunshine that mocked the shameful lamplight. She registered another night survived and prepared herself with nourishment, rigorous grooming and outrageous earrings to face another day.

She had switched on Radio 3 as an accompaniment to breakfast but something of the previous evening's restlessness remained, and she felt disinclined to concentrate on anything for very long. She wanted to pace up and down while she sorted out her priorities. A few miles' tramp, or even two or three turns round the room, and she felt sure she would know what to do about Frank, her career prospects and the universe in general.

Suddenly, tears were rolling down her face and she beat the arm of the wheelchair in angry frustration. Then the radio music was followed by a news bulletin, reminding her that the world was full of trouble, most of it worse than her own. She continued her morning routine, rewashing her face, thankful at least that her skin was still young enough for the eye area to bear no traces of scrubbing.

She was carrying her breakfast tray back to the kitchen when the doorbell rang. Something bulky and interesting in the post? The morning was improving. But it was not a postman's uniform she could see through the frosted-glass panel in the door. She opened it to Rob Cameron.

Last night he had worn thigh-high waders and a scarlet wet suit to manhandle her in and out of the canoe. Now he was resplendent in a many-hued track suit. She thought he looked alien, untamed, but his manners were impeccable. Having checked that his visit was not inconvenient to her, he came in and, for a moment or two, they made polite small talk. When this did not explain his appearance, Zoe asked, with her customary frankness, 'What have you come for?'

He took the chair she indicated. 'To discuss certain misgivings I have...'

Zoe was very disappointed. She thought she had acquitted herself well the previous evening and that he had been favourably impressed with her efforts. It was important to her that she had impressed him. She was not going to be dismissed without a fight and faced Cameron aggressively. 'So, what are these misgivings?'

He was obviously ill at ease. 'Well, a bit nebulous and all to do with the kind of man Graham was. But you did say that you'd been a police officer and, last night in the pub, you seemed interested in what had happened, so I thought at least you'd hear me out.'

Zoe realized she had misinterpreted him again. Her spirits rose and, her voice considerably friendlier, she demanded, 'So, what kind of man was he?'

'Not the sort to carry out a series of pirouettes as his contribution to a rodeo...'

'What's a rodeo?'

Cameron grinned. 'Basically, it's a showing-off contest for clever and agile canoeists. The Yorkshire and Humberside region are hoping to organize one at the beginning of December.'

'And a pirouette?'

'You need an eddy line to give you the right conditions—the weir, for example. If the towback is longer than the canoe...' Zoe let him continue, hoping the technical terms would sort themselves out. 'You paddle towards the face of the stopper and get drawn in. The nose dips, the bow is raised and the boat stands on end. If it fails and the nose catches the deep water, the boat turns over in a somersault, but, if you do a half-turn in the air, it lands the right way up. That's a pirouette. It needs a lot of practice.'

'It needs a death wish!' They both paused, assimilating the significance of Zoe's remark. She hoped nothing in their later conversation would depend on her precise understanding of the manoeuvre. 'So, you think Crowther couldn't have done it? I thought he was one of your coaches.'

Cameron shook his head. 'He was a supervisor, very willing and quite useful, but he hadn't even got the basic qualification of instructor. He just kept an eye on the beginners on flat water, repeated to them what he'd heard me say, and was prepared to fish out anyone who got into difficulties. Doing that and giving the kids the impression that he'd been the Shaun Baker of his generation kept him happy. If he was invited to demonstrate, he'd shake his head and say it was time for their hour of glory now and that he'd had his day, unless the club ever really needed him.'

Zoe realized suddenly that her hospitality was wanting. 'I haven't offered you coffee!'

He grinned. 'I was hoping you would.' He got up and opened the door for her as she propelled her chair towards the kitchen. Her glance rebuked him but, having now addressed the subject that had preoccupied him last evening, he dealt with her ungraciousness very directly. 'I know the disabled hate to be helped with things they can do. I don't know what's off limits for you—you'll have to guide me—but I would hope basic courtesy isn't ruled out.'

Zoe chuckled and busied herself with

cups whilst he leaned in the doorway, examining her kitchen with interest. She pointed out its distinguishing features good-humouredly, the cupboards three feet from the floor, the split cooker with both rings and oven just above the level of her knees, the sink at a similar height, the pipes underneath it lagged since she would not know if the hot one was burning her legs.

She plugged in the kettle. 'You'll notice all the power points are raised and the light switches lowered. You can't come in and help or there won't be room for the chair to turn round.' She realized she found him physically very attractive and decided that such proximity might not be wise. 'Go and clear a space for the tray on the coffee-table. Shove the things on to the floor.'

She called through to him as he obediently stacked files and papers. 'I'm lucky. The police paid for me to get this house and fix it. There was an act passed years ago, making local authorities responsible for meeting the housing needs of the disabled, but it was useless from the start because the assessment of the need is at *their* discretion!'

His thirst quenched, Cameron returned to the purpose of his visit and the subject of Graham Crowther. 'I took his offer with a pinch of salt. I didn't expect him to turn up and perform on the day.'

'But, if he was trying to make himself popular, wouldn't he be in worse standing with the club if he let them down than if he hadn't volunteered at all?' Zoe watched enviously as Cameron shovelled sugar into his cup.

'Oh, he'd have had some excuse ready, having to work, some crisis at home. I even thought he might deliberately injure himself in some minor way, hoping to get sympathy for missing his great moment.'

'Didn't you like him?'

Cameron waved his expressive, long-fingered hands as he tried to define his feelings, and Zoe deliberately averted her eyes from them. 'I liked him, I was impatient with him, I was sorry for him—I don't know. What I do know is that he was something of a physical coward and was ashamed of it. His stories were to try to prevent the other members despising him as he despised himself.'

'Why did he?'

'I don't know. I wasn't his father confessor, I just canoed with him, but he did talk to me more than to the others. It was probably due to having to live with his vile-tongued cow of a wife. It would be interesting to talk to someone who knew him before he married her. She constantly belittled and criticized him so he had to compensate with grandiose tales. He was a bad liar. His stories were too far-fetched and he over-estimated what the other club members were prepared to believe.'

'Was it just about canoeing that he told his stories?'

Cameron hesitated. 'Well, it was to me, but I've heard the others giggling about some tale of a previous job and how he saved his firm from bankruptcy, and I think he put it about that he was a great one for the girls before he made his choice and became a faithful husband.'

Zoe glanced at her watch reluctantly. 'My first client today is at half-eleven. I don't want to be rude but can you come to the point? What exactly are you trying to suggest?'

Cameron shook his head and studied his fingernails. 'Exactly? I don't know. I'm not happy that the police have come to the right conclusion. I don't think Graham went to the river on Sunday morning to practice rodeo stunts. I don't believe he had the bottle to overreach himself and die attempting one trick too many.

'For a start, he wouldn't have broken the basic rule that you don't go on the water alone to try something risky. He always covered up his timidity by sticking strictly to the safety code, "to set the younger members a good example". He'd have been meticulous about buoyancy aids too. He always used a high-volume kayak that has solid buoyancy as well as airbags, and he always checked the airbags before he went on the water. He was wearing a waistcoat with inflatable panels. It was damaged when we found him but there was enough air in it to have been some help to him. *And* he was an excellent swimmer.'

He began gathering up the cups. 'You wash these and I'll dry them. I'd dry them if you could walk. I'd even do it if you could walk on your hands.'

She took the loaded tray from him but indicated with a jerk of her head that he might follow and squeeze into the kitchen. 'I could, too. I was quite a reasonable gymnast.' She ran water into the bowl. 'Have you any positive ideas? What do you think is a likelier scenario?' He dried cups assiduously without answering. 'Are you suggesting Crowther committed suicide?' He placed the clean cups on the work surface, still silent. 'Or do you think someone helped him on his way?'

He muttered, 'I wouldn't put it past her.'

Zoe poured away the soapy water before turning to him severely. 'I gathered earlier that you don't care for his wife, but you can't throw wild accusations about like that. I take it you haven't made them to the police. Why aren't you talking to them?'

'They wouldn't listen—well, they did, but it didn't make any difference. They said there was no evidence to prove it wasn't an accident.'

Zoe knew only too well that lack of manpower in the Cloughton force had led to a less than thorough investigation of some sudden deaths. There were often more urgent matters to attend to than the preparation of a case of malicious intent when it had little chance of being proven. The police were not necessarily happy with the coroner's decision. 'So what, if anything, do you want me to do?'

Cameron twisted the damp tea-cloth unhappily between his fingers. 'I don't know what you can do. I just think that Graham has been tucked away too tidily and I can't go along with the people who want to gloss it over.'

'Do you think he killed himself?'

'No! That's the only thing I am sure of. He thought the world was coming to an end if he got a bruise or a scratch. He might have been guilty of a multitude of sins, but not that one. He would never have deliberately and seriously damaged himself.'

The doorbell rang, followed immediately by clattering in the hall and Frank's voice, teasing and cheerful. 'Chatting up my woman, Rob, while my back is turned? Zoe, I've got a couple of tickets for the Rep on Saturday, courtesy of the grateful owner of a patient. I'll trade one of them for a cup of that coffee I can smell.' He came in, stopped and stared, mesmerized by the drying-cloth in Cameron's hand. Then his lips tightened. 'Forget the coffee. I haven't time. Do you want to see this play?'

Wordlessly, Zoe nodded.

'Then I'll collect you at half-past six.' He saluted them curtly and was gone.

Zoe was not sure whether Cameron understood the significance of the small exchange. She was grateful that he hung the cloth to dry without comment and dragged her mind back to their abandoned conversation. 'There are several things I could do. To begin with it would be useful to know exactly what the police have done and what they're thinking.'

'Would they still tell you?'

Zoe shrugged. 'If they won't tell me, they might tell the wheelchair. It makes people feel guilty, especially policemen. They have great difficulty refusing it. Using the information I might get from them and what the club members can tell us, we could try to reconstruct

64

Crowther's weekend and possibly identify this mysterious angler who was seen on the bank on Sunday morning.'

'Will you do it?'

Zoe thought she was still considering the question but her head was nodding. Possibly she would have agreed to almost anything he asked her.

'We ought to find out about Linda's weekend...'

Zoe's tone was sharp. 'I said that I'd look into the business, not that I'd try to prove that she was responsible!'

'She really hated him.'

'And you really hate her?'

Cameron ignored the question. 'She hated him most of all because he wouldn't let her have the child put away.'

Chapter Five

Zoe sat in her office on Friday afternoon, making a mental list of questions for her own consideration. The first—was Linda Crowther going to turn up for her appointment?—would be answered in less than five minutes. The rest were more difficult. Did she want to investigate the death of her client's husband, and was it wise? The former she had answered to Rob Cameron, answered in the affirmative in spite of her misgivings. And the fact that she had misgivings suggested that the investigation was definitely unwise, particularly if she wanted to continue working for Relate.

She thought she did. Lately, as she became more skilled in the techniques she had been taught, she had gained a great deal of satisfaction from helping to free the logjam of resentments and fears that had inhibited and worried her various clients. The work had come relatively easily to her, akin as it was to her police experience with victims of assault and rape and with domestic disputes which had flared up to make police intervention necessary.

She had often thought, as she attended these 'domestics', that a bit of trained guidance, offered much earlier in the disputes, would have prevented violence. The conviction had led her, in her enforced leisure, to Relate. She knew it had been this experience, as well as her steady relationship with Frank, that had persuaded the staff to take her on and train her. She thought back through the instruction she had received, trying and failing to remember any command that expressly forbade a Relate counsellor to function as a private detective, concentrating in both capacities on the same poor woman. Nevertheless, she had grave doubts about the ethics of the undertaking.

It would not be easy to be fair to Linda Crowther, nor to be relaxed and natural in her dealings with her. Zoe decided to take things a step at a time. She would ask no investigative questions during the counselling. It could hardly be wrong just to listen. Besides, Mrs Crowther probably would not show up again. In that case, she could approach her in future wearing just the one hat. But the intercom buzzed and her colleague's voice announced the lady's arrival.

Today, Mrs Crowther was not so much wearing the black leather jacket as taking refuge inside it. She undid the buttons but then wrapped it more closely round herself as she cut short Zoe's commiserations, leaned forward and asked, 'Will you come to the funeral? You're the only person I've ever been honest with about my marriage, the only one who can have any idea of how I feel. It's on Tuesday at the crematorium.' Zoe considered and her client quickly took offence. 'Don't worry, it's not important. I shouldn't have asked. I realize it's above and beyond what you're paid for.'

Zoe was needled. 'But we're not! Paid, I mean, and I'm not unwilling to be there. I was just trying to remember if there's wheelchair access. I've learned not to take for granted my right to visit where I please.' When her client had the grace to blush, if not to apologize, Zoe was satisfied. 'I certainly know something of how you felt about your husband when he was alive. Tell me how you feel now.'

Mrs Crowther was belligerent. 'Am I supposed to say "guilty"—or "triumphant", maybe? After all, I did say I wanted to be rid of him and now I seem to have managed it.' Just the lead-in she wanted. Zoe resisted it only after a hard struggle.

'Never mind what you're supposed to say. What do you feel?'

'Enormous relief.' The relief seemed to increase as a result of being admitted to. 'I'll never have to sleep with him any more.

68

He'll never again sit close to me on the sofa and say, "Let's make love tonight." What a silly phrase—though none of the scientific terms or other euphemisms would have averted the distaste I always felt at the idea.' She gave Zoe a shamefaced grin. 'I always made a list of conditions. He had to shave and shower immediately before he got into bed with me, partly because that made it slightly less disgusting and partly because I thought making it a lot of trouble would put him off.'

'And it didn't?'

Linda sighed. 'I got so that I could run through the routine as I do with any domestic task required of me: the satin nightdress, the perfume. I specially hated him pulling clumsily at my nightdress. Once that was off I could disengage my mind till the rest was over.'

Making her tone carefully neutral, Zoe asked, 'Was it sex with Graham that horrified you, or the idea of sexual relations with any man?'

'Are you asking me if I'm a lesbian?'

'Not necessarily, but I'd be interested to know if you've given the idea any consideration.'

She considered it now, dispassionately. 'I'm not sure. I've certainly never considered a physical relationship with a woman. I suppose I didn't get accustomed

69

to touching at the age most other people did. My mother used to boast about leaving me to cry in my cot. She refused to "spoil" me by picking me up whenever I demanded attention. The only times I remember her touching me were when she smacked me for being naughty. I'm sure she had serious problems of her own.'

'What did being naughty consist of?'

The question left Mrs Crowther at a loss. 'I'm not sure, but being good meant doing as I was told without demur, being sycophantically obliging to all her acquaintances and keeping clean and quiet. Later, I had to bring home exemplary school reports that she could pass round the family. I wasn't to talk about school, though, or later about university. The family must never think I was a show-off.'

'Did you get positive pleasure out of your mother's approval—and your teachers?'

'I don't know. I thought something unspeakably awful would happen if I lost it.'

'How did you get on with other children?'

She considered and decided, sadly, 'They bore with me. They couldn't like or dislike me because I wasn't a proper person. I had no idea what I wanted, what I was genuinely interested in, even who I was, except a very clear idea that I was my mother's daughter. I longed for university and the great adventure of self-discovery but I only found that I'd taken my "home" self to college. Work posed no problems but I formed no real relationships. It was a women's college—what else?'

Mrs Crowther's manner was beginning to change and, with it, Zoe's attitude towards her. She was exploring her childhood with trepidation, still giving a fluent account but only, Zoe thought, because thinking in an orderly sequence seemed to come naturally to her. She began to wonder if her client's problems were too serious and of too long standing to be dealt with by such an amateur as herself. She realized that the narrative was continuing and tuned in again.

'After finals, I decided to teach. It was the only career I could think of and teachers were the only professionals I'd met.'

'And how did that work out?'

'Surprisingly well. Although I dreaded confrontations with assertive pupils, I could make my subject interesting and it usually suited them to listen. In those days, most of them still wanted to learn.'

After a long silence, Zoe asked, 'So when did Graham come on the scene?'

'We met on teaching practice. I was glad

he had a girl-friend and pretended I had just a casual relationship of my own. Then he had his big break-up with Shirley. It was second nature to me to take him under my wing. I only wanted Brownie points for being a useful crutch, but he probably thought I was giving him the come-on. I wasn't bad-looking, and soon he seemed smitten.'

'How did you feel about that?'

She stared at her knees. 'Mixed up. A peck on the cheek made me feel normal. I had a boy-friend. This was what other girls did. But sometimes he put his tongue in my mouth and that felt dirty and invasive. When we parted, he held me against him and his thing—I couldn't bring myself to name it even in my own mind—pressed against me in an embarrassing fashion. I didn't know what to do. By then I was becoming desperate to be normal. I thought if I could get used to it, perhaps I would react differently. Besides, I'd been taught to be obliging so I tried hard not to recoil. Submission I found I could manage but the desired response was beyond me. I could tell he was puzzled.

'He can't have been terribly highly sexed himself, or he'd surely have dropped me. Instead, while we were out for a walk, he dismayed me by asking me to marry him. I panicked. It would be impolite to refuse but the idea terrified me. I muttered something about the rest of our lives being a long time, and hoped he'd have second thoughts, forget about it, but he asked again and again.'

Her story proceeded jerkily. Zoe controlled her urge to comment, reassure, ask further questions. Her client seemed to have forgotten she had an audience, and was just thinking and remembering aloud.

'I mumbled platitudes, put him off. I dreaded our walks after that. I couldn't enjoy the sun and the wind and the scrambling, because, when we got out of breath and sat down, his hands violated me. Looking back, his overtures were probably tentative, even apologetic, but they were violation to me.

'He seemed to accept my total lack of response. I wonder now what on earth he was thinking, but at the time my mind was swamped with panic, no part of it free to wonder about him, except to remember that, sometime, he was going to spring that question again.'

There was a long pause before she finished her account. 'When it did come, I couldn't bring myself to offend him by refusing again. Suddenly, I found myself engaged, like poor Mr Polly.'

What, Zoe wondered, would a psychiatrist do for her client? Didn't they try to dredge up the reasons for people's inhibitions, get their patients to understand themselves? This patient had done all that for herself but it hadn't helped her much. She brought her attention back to the continuing monologue.

'At least I wasn't infertile and I do have some feeling for Peter. I tried to leave him free, to let him make his own choices, short of putting him in danger or encroaching too much on the rights of others. It seems to have worked. As far as I can gather he has plenty of friends, maybe healthy physical relationships. I don't ask. But I made Graham's life as much of a mess as mine. If I hadn't married him, perhaps we could both have been happy.'

'Are you sure you weren't? All right, there was plenty of irritations on the surface that absorbed your immediate attention, but you stayed together. There must have been something...'

Zoe was silenced by her client's expression. The idea of her marriage having been at least good in parts seemed to cause her pain, or was it puzzlement? After a while Mrs Crowther said, 'I'll have to think about that, perhaps for next time. I didn't mean to say all this today. I was going to tell you about Sunday.'

Zoe smiled to herself. 'All things come to he who waits' had been much quoted by her mother. This was the very first manifestation of a truth she had always rejected as a lie. Having resisted the temptation to cross-question Mrs Crowther about her doings on the previous Sunday, she was being doubly rewarded. Her client had volunteered the answer to the outstanding question left over from her first session—how she had come to marry her husband—and now she was offering an account of how she had spent the day of her husband's death.

'Sunday?'

'Yes, I chose it for my day out. My mother picked Helena up on Saturday night. On Sunday I went off to do my own thing as you suggested. I got up early and thought I'd left Graham in bed. That was one of the things we'd always rowed about, that I wanted to make good use of the day and he waited until it was imperative to get up and he could only be at work or wherever in time by rushing bad-temperedly about.'

'So you didn't sleep together on Saturday night. Had you quarrelled?'

'Sort of. Someone rang and Graham wanted to go out for a drink with whoever it was. I didn't really want to go out, but I was annoyed not to be included. In the end, Graham refused and arranged something else with the person instead.

For once he flared up. After all I was going out without him all of the next day. I slammed off to bed and he slept in the spare room.'

'So you didn't meet on Sunday morning?'

'No, and I didn't find his note until I came back on Sunday evening, and then there were two policemen waiting for me. I found it on the floor when they'd gone. It must have been caught up in a draught.

'To get back to Sunday, I planned to drive up river past the clubhouse and walk along the path to Denham Clough, so I was only a mile or so from where it happened.'

'Walking was what you wanted?'

'Being on my own was what I wanted to begin with. When your upbringing has taught you that you're only acceptable when you're pretending to be other than who and what you are, you can only begin to be yourself when there's nobody there to pretend to. It was a beautiful morning. That distracted me for a while. Then I just walked and let my mind run free.

'I deliberately tried not to think about my parents or Graham or the children. I began to remember my schooldays. I loved school. Being there made me feel I could be or do just about anything. My teachers seemed to know me better than my family did.

'I had lunch at a riverside pub, all the things that I love and Graham hates so we never have. Avocado and roast beef. Graham was convinced that if food was enjoyable it must be harmful and that a few grams of fat would seize up his heart.

'Whilst I was eating, I heard people talking in the bar about police activity and a body in the river?'

'Did you have any fears for your husband?'

'I never thought about Graham being anywhere near. I assumed he wouldn't roll out of bed till lunchtime without me to nag and prod him into activity. I went to see a film in the afternoon. *Blue Moon* it was called, but don't ask me what it was about. I sat in comfortable warmth, still thinking about the schoolgirl I had been, trying to recapture all the dreams and ambitions I'd had then. When I came out, I suddenly wanted to go home.'

'Did you?'

'No. I hadn't answered enough questions. It was dark, so I couldn't walk any more. I had tea in the cinema café, then on the spur of the moment I went into a church I was passing. I prayed there wouldn't be a sermon. I'd escaped all day from having to be a good daughter, good wife, good mother, and I hoped to escape an exhortation to be a good Christian, at least till I'd discovered whether that was what I wanted. When it became obvious there was to be a good dose of hellfire, I slipped out. Then I did go home and found two police officers waiting for me.'

She smiled at Zoe, triumphantly. 'When they'd gone I went to fetch Helena. I felt so strong after a day on my own that I managed to stand up to my parents. I refused to stay at their house and forbade my mother to come back with me to mine. They did persuade me to leave Helena for another night, so I had twelve more hours on my own.' She fell silent.

Zoe watched her, speculatively. Such pride over such a small gesture of self-assertion. Where would this woman have found the resolution to kill someone? As Rob had said of Graham, she might be guilty of a multitude of sins but surely not this one.

Linda blinked and began speaking again. 'I didn't ring Peter until Monday. I had to think how to break the news to him.'

'Did you think of a way to break it gently?'

'That wasn't the problem. I thought he'd accuse me of killing Graham. And he did!'

When Linda Crowther had left, a light tap on Zoe's door heralded the arrival of her immediate superior. Laura Gibson was elegantly ageless and even the forthright Zoe dared not hazard a guess, still less a question. A navy wool blazer was draped over her shoulders above white sweater and slacks, creaseless and unmarked. The rest of the staff wondered how she managed it. Zoe knew and admired Laura's time-consuming commitment.

She perched on the edge of Zoe's desk, ignoring the clients' chairs. 'How did you get on last night?'

Zoe grimaced. 'Depends what you mean. I survived. I didn't drown anyone else. I got a bit wet and extremely cold.' She grinned suddenly. 'Actually, I did rather well. I'm looking forward to the next session.'

Laura adjusted the collar of her elegant jacket and shook her head. Zoe smiled as this movement caused a tress of blond-streaked, chin-length hair to tangle with drop ear-rings. No one was perfect, not even Laura.

'Well, each to her own. What put the idea into your head?'

Zoe's nose wrinkled. 'Partly the challenge, I suppose. I always enjoyed physical activities and I mean to go on with them.

And Frank's got very keen. If we're to stay together we've got to have some common interests. Our musical tastes don't overlap.' It occurred to her that at least they used the same criteria to make judgements on it. Perhaps that counted for something.

'He's an expert then?'

'Oh, no. He's only about one stage in front of me. We're starting equal, more or less. Frank's always ready to try winter activities that will keep him in trim till the cricket season starts again, but I think he's enjoying it for its own sake now.'

Laura abandoned the hard corner of the desk and slid into one of the marginally more comfortable chairs. 'I hope it isn't the cautionary tales you hear in here that put you off marrying him.' Zoe shook her head and remained silent. Laura persevered. 'I supposed it's—well, the obvious problems?'

Zoe was always amused by the varying degrees of directness and politeness with which people enquired about her sexual prowess. 'Passive but adequate,' would have been her answer to anyone who deserved an answer at all. She knew that one of the important issues to be resolved was Frank's guilt at taking his pleasure, a pleasure she was denied, at her expense. She had given him simple instructions: 'Learn all over again to give me what pleasure I can enjoy.' Their coupling was not for her the dutiful routine that Frank imagined. They had experienced a satisfying physical relationship before the accident that Zoe could enjoy in retrospect when he approached her now. Some paraplegics claimed still to enjoy sex but Zoe was convinced that for them, as for her, it was a mixture of memory and imagination. She hoped her memory would remain clear and her imagination vivid. She recollected vaguely a race of creatures in one of C.S Lewis's science fiction novels who all experienced sexual intercourse just once. All their life before it was a preparation for it and life afterwards was—what? An anticlimax? She couldn't remember now, nor which book it all came from. It suddenly occurred to her that the creatures must have been incredibly fertile.

Realizing that Laura had taken her silence to mean she was offended, Zoe hastened to continue the conversation without too drastic a change of subject. 'I can never work out how much Frank's attitude towards me has changed since the accident. When I'm depressed I wonder if he sees me as one of the broken, wounded creatures that it's his mission in life to restore.'

'But he first proposed to you before your accident.'

'That's another question I have to keep in mind. If I'd met him afterwards, I'd be the girl in a wheelchair that he'd fallen in love with. I don't want him to marry a memory of the girl I used to be.'

'But that's...'

'Inconsistent? I know. Knowing doesn't help. Anyway, I thought you'd come to ask about Linda Crowther.'

Normally Zoe was glad that the confidentiality required of Relate's counsellors towards the information disclosed to them did not apply between the counsellors themselves. They met often to share the problems of each other's clients and offer suggestions about the best advice to give. Today she wanted the discussion with Laura to be minimal and knew it was because she was withholding information from her.

'How are you getting on with her?'

'She's using me for some odd purpose of her own. It's particularly clear to me when, occasionally, she's diverted from that purpose by something that occurs to her actually in the course of our discussion—for example the idea of her husband being the one to take the responsibility for a split between them and having an affair.

'She suddenly realized then that, if he had the power to attract someone else, she wouldn't despise him so much. She's written him off because she has so little sense of self-worth. She feels the sort of man who'd settle for her is even more contemptible than she is. And yet, behind all that there is an enormous conceit—an idea that she could have taken the world by storm, if only the world had not been so mean and uncooperative.

'What have most of our clients done to deserve all the time we spend on them? They seem to think they have a right to permanent happiness and well-being, and they're chiefly unhappy just because they sit and expect. You don't have customers who've slipped in between stints of charity work, or shopping for neighbour.'

'I do, actually, though I understand what you're saying. You've faced a good deal of trauma but it was your body that was damaged, not your self-worth. Are you telling me you've had enough of us here?'

Zoe was shocked at where her tongue had led her. 'I don't know what I'm telling you. I applied for training because I could see that most of the domestic violence I was called to deal with could have been avoided if the people concerned in it had had chance to work out their differences calmly a long time before.'

'And what's changed your mind?'

'It isn't changed. It's just that the people

who resort to violence aren't the ones who come for advice. We get people with a compulsion to talk about themselves, an obsession with studying themselves. I don't know how to reach the people who really need help; how to avoid just humouring the self-obsessed.'

'Haven't they got a problem too?'

'I suppose so, but not one that I'm sympathetic to.'

'Mightn't ignoring it lead to violence in the end?' That, Zoe thought, was exactly what she was trying to find out. 'What are you telling me about Linda Crowther, in and amongst all this?' Laura added with a wry smile.

'I just want to tell her that everyone else has troubles too, most considerably worse than hers.'

'She isn't ready to hear it yet. Put me in the picture.'

Zoe described succinctly the essence of her client's complaints. 'I gather they were two insecure people each trying to use the other as a prop instead of trying to bolster the other up. She never even mentioned her kids till I asked. She exonerates her mother, can see she had problems of her own...'

'Probably because, with hindsight, and the irritation geographically removed, she can see more clearly. She'll remember all her husband's virtues, very likely, when she's had a few days to forget the irritations of his actual company. How much has the handicapped child affected them—or the absence of the clever one, now that he's away studying? You might explore that next time.'

'You think she'll carry on coming?'

'Probably. She's got a lot of anger screwing her up. I imagine she'll want to go on talking till she's exhausted it. I can put her with someone else, though.'

'No! Please leave her with me.'

Laura gave Zoe a long hard look before she left.

Chapter Six

On Sunday morning, the spell of strangely warm weather broke. Icy patches on the road had made Zoe's journey to church slower than usual, but she still had time to pause and admire the frost-rimmed holly leaves on the bushes between the graveyard and the car-park. Then the chill drove her indoors.

She propelled herself into church by the ramp that had caused such dissension between herself and her mother. She would write to the church council to thank them for its construction, she had told her parents belligerently, when some other member of the congregation wrote similarly in appreciation of the stone steps by which they took it for granted they should enter. The 'new' vicar, now four years into his incumbency at St Oswald's, had also offered to arrange for the widening of any of the doors she might wish to use.

He had not asked for her thanks and she knew it was unreasonable of her to feel resentment against him just because her mother was appalled that Zoe might be thought ungrateful and ill-mannered. Even more unfair was her grudge against him because the ramp, with its obnoxiously twee railing, ruined the comfortably solid shape of the Victorian building. Its substantial doors had fortunately proved wide enough to admit her wheelchair without any further desecration on her account.

She proceeded down the aisle to the side chapel adjacent to the choir stalls. Her place in the choir was accessible to her from there by a smaller, unobtrusive wooden ramp, the vicar's idea again. She really was an ungrateful bitch, she supposed. In a minute, whoever arrived first in the choir vestry at the foot of another flight of steps would come up to bring her her cassock, surplice and hymnbook. This morning, by a happy chance, it was Jerry Hunter, DS Hunter of the Cloughton CID.

He was a copper who always played by the rule-book, Zoe reflected ruefully, but she had various advantageous cards to play in her dealings with him. He was the person who had introduced her to the chamber choir which had since been her joy. Their views were identical on the new vicar, his alterations to the church building and the 'decline' he had brought about in the church music.

In addition, being a chauvinist (though not, she decided generously, a chauvinist pig), he felt personally guilty that his colleagues had allowed her to risk her life on duty in such ungentlemanly fashion. His attitude had enraged her when they worked together but she was happy to exploit it now. She even submitted to his tentative efforts to arrange the cassock tidily behind her, amused that her fear of being patronized was far exceeded by his fear of actually touching her.

He hovered awkwardly, not knowing how to leave her politely. Zoe bit back her irritation. Before her accident they had had a perfectly workable relationship. She had despised him, disapproved of the inhibiting way he had raised his unhealthily obedient children and the contemptible way he humoured his wife. He had been a little afraid of Zoe's forthright tongue and had avoided her company, except as a working colleague, where he had had occasion to commend her and had done so generously. Now, he made a point of chatting to her in an embarrassed fashion, pretending to enjoy her company in case he was thought wanting in charity towards the halt and the lame. She rescued him. 'Hadn't you better be robing yourself?' And, as he departed with relief, 'I'd appreciate a quiet word after the service.'

He forced a smile. 'Surely. I'll look out for you.' She noticed he looked worried. Did he think she wanted him to wangle a job for her? Already she regretted the approach to him. After their conversation he would go home with a troubled conscience for passing on a minute amount of information carefully chosen to be of the least possible use to her.

The appearance of Zoe's chair, lining itself up alongside the choir pews, was a sign to the congregation that the procession of the clergy and the rest of the choir was about to appear. The subdued chattering stopped. Those kneeling in devout attitude on lumpy hassocks returned their buttocks to the hard pews and rubbed the circulation back into knees patterned with the WI's cross-stitch.

Awake my soul and with the sun
Thy daily course of duty run.

Zoe joined enthusiastically in the first hymn which, for once, was out of the traditional hymnbook with traditional organ accompaniment. Free from the irritation of the banal repetitions and gratuitous syncopation of the vicar's usual choice of 'opening song', Zoe concentrated on the words she was singing. They were salutary.

Redeem thy misspent time that's past.
Live each day as if t'were thy last...

Was pumping Sergeant Hunter for confidential information, to which she no longer had right of access, a suitable occupation for her projected last day? This was a tall order from the God she alternately consulted and ignored. Zoe felt more comfortable with hymns that dwelt on the nature of God than on the nature of her responsibility to Him.

She wished she hadn't made the approach to Hunter. She was a definite ex-constable, no longer in the club. Having once been of the brotherhood didn't count with Jerry Hunter, in spite of the wheelchair being a guilt-producer, carrying a suggestion of the harmlessness, the impotence of its occupant. For DS Hunter, rules were rules.

Benny Mitchell would have been a better option. He was a free thinker like herself, always in trouble with his immediate superior for achieving what was required by the shortest possible route, which usually meant a deviation from protocol. Like her, he believed the end justified the means.

The hymn continued to mock her.

Let all thy converse be sincere,
Thy conscience as the noonday clear...

Church was good for the soul, bad for the

self-approbation. It was not often that her conscience bothered her. She was confident in her view of the world and her ability to deal with it. Now, though, she saw herself acting illogically. She had acceded to Rob Cameron's request because his view supported hers, bolstering up her groundless suspicion that Linda Crowther had in some way caused her husband's death. Her sole evidence was a carelessly used expression, 'I need to get rid of my husband,' followed swiftly by a report that the said husband was conveniently dispatched. That and the feeling that she was a pawn in some game that Linda Crowther was playing.

Confession, canticles, readings and creed passed unnoticed by Zoe and she sang her part in the anthem on automatic pilot. As the choir resumed their seats, she came to a decision. This afternoon, provided that he was prepared to welcome her, she would go to see Benny Mitchell. Now she had something to occupy her mind for the rest of the service. What excuse could she manufacture for having wanted to speak to Jerry?

Frank, having delivered with his usual fluency and resonance the portion of Genesis 3 assigned to him as lesson reader, was paying marginally less attention to the rest of the service than Zoe. Between his face and his service book floated a picture of Rob Cameron, comfortably ensconced in Zoe's kitchen, white teeth flashing in honey-brown face, tea-cloth in hand, his assistance being casually accepted like that of a long-standing husband.

And Zoe had seemed strangely abstracted just recently. She was up to something and she had no intention of sharing it with him. He strongly suspected that Cameron was in her confidence about whatever it was. Certainly it all dated from the evening of Zoe's introduction to canoeing.

Zoe was looking forward to her visit to the Mitchells, and not only because she hoped it would help her sort out her attitude to Linda Crowther.

She liked Benny and his family. Typically, he had made his inspector's daughter pregnant when she was less than half-way through her Oxford degree. Just as typically, he had made his peace with her family, not by abject apology but by being the sort of husband Virginia needed, encouraging her studies and taking responsibility for the children to an extent that allowed her not only to complete her first degree but also to embark on an MA course.

With all Benny's help, life could not have

been easy for Virginia. Their small son had been followed by a smaller daughter and much of her studying had been done with a baby in her lap whilst the nappies she had washed dried round her.

Zoe was disappointed when Benny answered the door and announced that he was by himself. The little boy, Declan, was mischievous and amusing; Caitlin, the toddler, a tomboy, threatening to outdo her brother in devilment; and Virginia herself was one of the very few people who treated Zoe now exactly as she always had.

It was a smallish house. She entered it by the wide and stepless back door after Benny had removed a pushchair, a tricycle and a large box of toys. Apart from these, the rooms showed little sign that a young family lived in them, though there were lightish patches on the carpets and chairs, probably the result of unspeakable stains being swiftly scoured from them. Zoe knew that the almost painful neatness and cleanliness was demanded and largely achieved by Benny. He had been the fifth child in a family of six who had all lived in a house far smaller than this one. The habits necessitated by his childhood had remained with him.

Sitting, minutes later with a steaming cup of coffee in her hand, Zoe was slightly less sorry for Virginia's absence.

She remembered Ginny's coffee! Benny sprawled at the end of the sofa opposite the television set and she hoped he was not silently regretting a missed rugby match as he demanded the reason for her visit. 'Not that you're not welcome at all times, but this was rather a last-minute arrangement.'

Faced with explaining her mission, Zoe suddenly found it seemed a ludicrous one. She justified her suspicions as best she could, buoyed up because her inner conviction that Linda Crowther was guilty strengthened in proportion to the seeming weakness of the case against her. When Benny had remained silent for ten seconds after the end of her recital, she realized how greatly she had been depending on his support.

She sighed. 'I suppose it's hardly a convincing theory. Thanks for listening, anyway, and I know I can trust you to—'

Benny glared at her. 'For pity's sake, woman, shut up and let me think.' The silence continued for more than a minute apart from the small sounds of his refilling their cups. Zoe drank and waited, and as he drained his mug he seemed to come to a decision. 'I'm not happy about this drowning and I'm not the only one at the station to feel that way. If you're prepared to poke your nose into it, I'll help you as

94

much as I can. We were on it for just a day before we were pulled off.'

'Why?'

'Because the Super managed to say something definite for once. His usual line is "Look into it but keep it low-key," so that he can't be accused either of wasting too much manpower or of not following up something that ought to be investigated. It leaves us with an inquiry on our hands that we haven't the resources to cope with adequately. This time, though, he definitely told us to drop it. Whatever we might suspect, there wasn't going to be anything we could prove.'

'How did you know that after only a day?'

'We knew that there wouldn't be either the time or the manpower for the in-depth investigation that would be necessary.' Mitchell shrugged. 'Drownings are difficult. There's often an open verdict for lack of clinching evidence of foul play. Blunt injuries to a body can be sustained by bumping into an obstruction, hitting a craft or floating objects. Nothing short of injuries clearly *not* caused by these bumps would justify real suspicion.'

'But most of your officers had them all the same?'

'There weren't any serious head injuries,

so Crowther shouldn't have been unconscious. And yet there were no signs of scratches or bruises to his hands and arms.'

'You mean he doesn't seem to have made any effort to save himself?'

'That's right, and there wasn't any trace either of drink or drugs in his system.'

'You were on the case, then, just for that day?'

'I didn't see the body. I was off duty when it was found. I came on at two o'clock and I was sent down to the clubhouse to talk to some of the canoeists. I had a quick look round and had quite a chat to the coach. I've heard for myself all the guff he's been giving you.'

'You don't take him seriously?'

'I can't say one way or the other, but I'm not satisfied that we looked far enough into what he was saying. I wasn't satisfied before he even opened his mouth. I said as much to him, told him we couldn't go further officially at the moment but that a good many of us were keeping our eyes skinned. It was after that that he came on strong with his own ideas.'

Zoe chuckled. 'If you feel like that, I'm surprised you haven't been beavering about on your own account...or have you?'

He shook his head. 'We gave up on this case because there wasn't a lead to follow that was likely to give us court evidence, and because there's so much else on. You'll have read about most of it, those young girls assaulted in Heath Royd, five of them now. There's yet another series of raids on the chemists in town and then there's that nutter masquerading as a social worker and going round telling people their kids are on the at-risk register. And, when I'm off duty these days, I have to remember I've two kids at home and another on the way.' He cut short her congratulations. 'No one else knows about it yet so don't say anything. Especially don't say was it an accident and especially don't say it to Ginny.'

'OK. What else?'

'The wife comes in for a packet. He'd just bumped up his insurance quite steeply. Briefly, we considered suicide, that he'd provided for her and the kids and made an end of it. His wife said the extra insurance was because he'd just been diagnosed with mild angina and thought he should make extra provision for the family. If he had a heart attack she wouldn't be able to go out to work because of the little girl. We spoke to his GP, who confirmed the heart trouble. We also asked if he was depressed. He said not clinically, but in a general way he was always depressed. The canoeists agreed. They put it down to having to live with his wife.'

'She said *she* was depressed and definitely blamed him. Perhaps she was right and they never should have married.'

Mitchell held up his hand to stop her. 'I share your idea that his death may not have been a simple accident, rather than your suspicions of the wife. If she did have any responsibility for it, she's taking a big risk coming to talk to you for hours at a time. I'd have thought she'd have been afraid of slipping up, giving herself away.'

'Maybe, trapped in the wrong marriage and with a handicapped child, she got her kicks by living dangerously.' It struck Zoe that that was exactly what she was doing herself and that before long she would reveal either to Cameron that she was counselling his suspect, or to Laura Gibson that she was investigating her. Thank heaven for Benny, to whom she could reveal everything and who could be trusted to keep his mouth shut.

'What sort of a woman is she?' he wanted to know.

'Peculiar!' was all Zoe could come up with as an immediate answer. 'She doesn't have confrontations, she lets things happen. I could imagine her perhaps committing a cowardly murder—you know, where she set a trap and then went away and thought about something else until her victim was found conveniently dead. Then she'd reason that it wasn't her fault, because, if the victim hadn't been so stupid, he wouldn't have been caught. I couldn't see her shooting someone or sticking a knife in him or...'

'Or holding him underwater till he stopped breathing?'

'She might get someone to do it for her.'

'Another man, you mean? You think she wanted to get rid of Graham so that she could replace him?'

'No, that's the last thing she'd do. Unless all the stuff she gave me at her last counselling session was a blind. No, I don't believe it was. I believe that she's either asexual or so repressed that she can't tell the difference.'

'If she wanted to kill him, why should she come to you and risk raising your suspicions? Surely it would have been better to keep as low a profile as possible.'

'But Rob Cameron would still have suspected her. When he came to me, he knew nothing about my meeting with her but he felt strongly enough to try to persuade me to advise him, help him.' Another question occurred to Zoe. 'Why does everyone accept that Crowther was practising pirouettes? Was it just because he happened to be found below the weir?'

'His wife says he left a note saying that was what he intended. She read it and threw it away.'

'Did you find it?'

He shook his head. 'She can't remember exactly what happened to it. We asked her to let us have it if it turned up.' When Zoe glared at him, he added, 'Ginny doesn't hang on to *my* scribbled notes. I can't believe Mrs C suddenly killed her husband because twenty-odd years of submitting to his sexual advances suddenly became too much. We didn't turn up anything that might have acted as a trigger.'

Zoe disagreed. 'I think if you endure something for long enough you can suddenly snap without a precipitating factor—but not Linda. Her inability to do anything decisive is her chief problem. Her marriage problems are, to a certain extent, because she wanted Graham to be decisive for her and he either couldn't or wouldn't.' They drank in silence for a few moments, till Zoe volunteered, 'It was her doctor who sent her to me. It would be interesting to have a talk to him. He's obviously been in her confidence about their relationship for some time, and it's the same bloke who saw her through the second pregnancy. He'd be a useful witness on several counts.'

'Is that an offer?' Zoe nodded. 'I'm sure you could use the excuse of counselling her. Ask him why he referred her to you in the first place.'

'I'll try something like that. What else would you have done, given the chance?'

'A meticulous search of the contents of his locker in the clubroom—if they haven't been handed to his wife by now. We did have a quick look and it was all canoeing stuff. Then I'd have found excuses to talk to his work colleagues, his son, all the other canoeists. Oh, and I'd do my damnedest to find that angler. I can give you the address of the bloke who reported seeing him, so long as you only bump into him "by accident".'

'Maybe he was only pretending to be an angler, to have an excuse for being seen by the river.'

But Mitchell thought he was genuine. 'If you were buying a rod as a prop for a bit of play acting, you wouldn't choose a top-of-the-range Hardy, and I understand it isn't the sort of thing most people would be willing to lend. Though I suppose he could have borrowed and returned it without anyone knowing.'

When the coffee-pot was quite empty, Zoe reluctantly took her leave. 'I'm sorry to have taken up most of your precious afternoon's peace and quiet.'

He waved away her apologies. 'Nonsense, you've made my day. It was really bugging me that someone might have got away with murder.'

Chapter Seven

Zoe drew back her curtains on Monday morning to reveal the first proper November day of the year. Hood's poem floated through her mind.

No sun, no moon, no proper time o'
the day...
No fruits, no flowers, no leaves, no
birds.
November!

The houses across the road were merely a dark suggestion of substance, looming in drear mist. Clearer because nearer, her neighbour's cruelly pruned lime tree sulked dejectedly and his For Sale notice at the end of the garden leaned at a drunken angle and buried a corner of its garish lettering into his dripping privet hedge.

The scene reflected Zoe's mood. Her mind dwelt insistently and tiresomely on the death of a man she had never even met, and the possible involvement in it of his odd wife whom she had met only a couple of weeks ago and yet with whom she had become inextricably involved. She half wished Rob Cameron had never shared his suspicions with her. Perversely, she

103

felt little interest in the matter and yet she was utterly incapable of leaving it alone. And Cameron had inadvertently further complicated her already fraught relationship with Frank.

When the curtains were fully drawn back, the room was only marginally lighter. She decided to leave the table-lamp on. At least, last night, she had managed to keep the one in the bedroom off. Her mind had had no room for night terrors, being largely occupied with the questions arising from her visit to DC Mitchell. They had distracted her too from being good company for Frank all the previous evening. After their stilted conversation and stiff manner to each other during the disastrous Saturday theatre visit, relations between them were extremely fragile.

She was grateful that it was Frank's 'ops' day. She would not have to worry about an encounter with him until this evening, and she had no need till then to worry about his hurt and bewilderment. It would not intrude between him and his anaesthetized animals.

The doorbell rang, announcing Cameron's arrival, and she was surprised by the great pleasure she felt at the prospect of a morning spent in his company. She examined it sternly, and opened the door, trying to reassure herself that it was due merely to relief that he could cope with both her disability and her mood.

She had rung him on her return from the Mitchells' house and now explained to him succinctly the information Benny had given her about the present police attitude to Crowther's death and his advice on their own next moves.

Cameron listened attentively. Then he lifted the carrier-bag he had brought in with him on to his knee and regarded her sheepishly. 'I can help with the contents of the locker. I was down at the club fairly early on the Sunday morning, though I wasn't the first. It was a couple of the under-fifteens who found the body. Ken Hammond had taken them out. His own kid was throwing up all over the place, so he sent the other down to the clubhouse to phone for an ambulance and the police. He knew I'd be there and he thought I'd have my mobile. I let the kid use it and meanwhile I whipped through Graham's locker.'

'So the boys recognized him in the water?'

'The tougher one was a girl, but yes, everyone at the club knew Graham in one capacity or another.'

'And why did you interfere with his locker?'

Cameron's tone was belligerent. 'He

105

used it as his hidey-hole. All the stuff he didn't want Linda to know about, he pushed to the back, in this bag behind his wet suit. I had my suspicions about what might be in it, so I stuffed it into my car boot. Young Kate did say they'd found "his body" but I was hoping then that he might still be alive and I knew he wouldn't want anyone else to find it.'

'If he'd been alive, no one would have looked in his locker, surely?'

Cameron shrugged. 'I just did it instinctively. He was the sort of bloke who needed protecting. Then, when the police did want to look round, I didn't like to admit that I'd rifled his locker. I didn't dare to, in fact, so I left the carrier where it was.'

Zoe was indignant. 'You've got a cheek, criticizing the police for coming to the wrong conclusions, then calmly announcing that you've been withholding vital evidence.'

Cameron looked defiant. 'You'd have done the same if you'd known him. Anyway, it wouldn't have brought him back to life and I'm doing my best for him now. Let's go through the stuff. You won't say...?'

Zoe was annoyed. 'I'm promising nothing except to do my best to find out if anyone is to blame for his death.'

Apparently satisfied with this, Cameron

upended the plastic bag on the table. They both contemplated the resulting small heap of cards, letters and papers, curious but reluctant to pry into them. Zoe, who had had to do it before, overcame her scruples first and drew out a yellow card. 'A Jennifer Lister recital at the Festival Hall! He was musical, then?'

Cameron frowned. 'Not so's you'd notice, though he did go to that Philharmonic concert at the Vic, the one Frank had to suffer in your place.' They both grinned. 'They had some CDs of folk and pop music in their racks at home but I always thought they were Peter's.'

Zoe shook her head. 'Jeffie doesn't sing pop music. More likely Purcell or Brahms or Stravinski.'

'"Jeffie?" Is that a nickname? She comes from round here, doesn't she? Do you know her?'

Zoe turned the ticket over thoughtfully. 'It makes a change from "Jenny". I know her vaguely, one of my school's distinguished old girls, a bit older than Frank and me. I wish it was my ticket. She's superb.'

Cameron was puzzled. 'I can't imagine Graham listening to serious music. He never hummed any that I recognized, or talked about music. Maybe he and Linda knew this Jennifer Lister in the past and

107

were going for old times' sake.'

Zoe thought not. 'If they were going together, why would he keep his ticket separate from hers?'

'You think he intended to go secretly? It's no crime to go to a concert. Why shouldn't he tell her?'

Zoe could think of several reasons. 'Because he was going to do a shady deal with someone in the interval? To meet another woman there? To...'

Cameron had examined the ticket for himself. 'He must have had a good reason for wanting to be there. This ticket cost twenty quid! You said you wanted to go. Why don't you use the ticket and see what happens?'

Zoe was taken aback at this high-handedness. 'But that's stealing. It belongs to his wife now. You aren't thinking straight anyway. I can't use a ticket for a seat in the middle of the stalls.'

Cameron neither blushed nor apologized, merely urged her impatiently. 'You said people couldn't refuse a wheelchair. Get them to swap it. Or, better still, get Frank to use this ticket and you beg one for yourself.'

Zoe shrugged. 'Considering the present state of our relationship, he probably won't take me anywhere, particularly not to another classical concert.'

'It's me, isn't it? I realized I'd put my foot in it the other day. He surely doesn't think...'

'I'm sure he doesn't think I want to swap him. He's just afraid that I'll waste the whole of the rest of our lives coming round to the idea that we can go on together as we were before the accident.'

'Why haven't you?'

Suddenly, Zoe saw the answer. 'Because we're not the same, either of us. He can only see that I've changed *my* attitude, but he's changed too. He's angry at the moment because I let you dry the dishes. I let you because you told me I was being ridiculous, that I was not only refusing unnecessary help but refusing to tolerate anything short of actual rudeness.' She cut short his protest. 'Your words were milder but that's what their tone told me.' She hoped this was an honest explanation but feared it might not be.

'Frank's never angry with me now. His tone, whenever he addresses me, varies between tender concern and sweet reason. I can't remember one occasion in the last two years when he's allowed himself to be furious with me, or flatly to contradict me. I can't spend the rest of my life being humoured, especially by Frank. I hate verbal pussyfooting! In hospital I much preferred the nurses who told me about their antics at the Saturday disco to the ones who tactfully vetted their bedside chat.' This had to be why she found talking with Rob so refreshing.

'I can see that. The ones who talked freely were telling you they didn't pity you.'

'That's right. And why should they?' She fished in the table drawer for a booklet which she handed to him. He saw it was a catalogue of aids for the disabled. 'When I look at some of the gadgets in there, I realize how small my handicap is.' Fearful that this smacked of 'brave little woman', she hurried on. 'Helping the disabled gain greater independence is big business nowadays. My mother has a love-hate relationship with that booklet. It shows that I can obtain all I need to be able to live alone, when her dearest wish is that I should either "settle down" with Frank or return to the maternal fold and be looked after there. Since she's eventually become convinced that I won't have either, she suggests that I get every device and gimmick on the market, whether I need it or not. But then she tut-tuts to my father about how ugly it all is and how it spoils the décor.'

Zoe smiled indulgently and picked up a card that revealed Graham Crowther's membership of a blue-film club in Leeds.

'Understandable, I suppose,' she observed without thinking. Cameron's expression was quizzical but he made no reply.

When their fingers touched, Zoe moved to the other side of the table. Together, the two sorted through the rest of the pile. Zoe examined a catalogue of very expensive canoeing equipment and a circular from the Inland Revenue before Cameron handed her a photograph. She scrutinized the small girl, stocky and overweight with round flat cheeks and slanting, puffy eyes. She seemed to have escaped the flat Down's nose, but the thick-lipped mouth hung open, the jawline was heavy and the neck almost non-existent.

Zoe handed back the picture. 'Did he have to hide away his pictures of his daughter?'

Cameron shook his head. 'Oh, no, there are pictures of both her and Peter around the house.'

There remained just a pale green envelope with a London postmark. It was addressed to Crowther and contained a short note. 'The ticket, as promised. Regards. L.G.'

'So, someone sent him the ticket and he didn't want Linda to see it. Does it look like a woman's handwriting, do you think?' Cameron handed the small green sheet over for Zoe's scrutiny.

111

She shook her head. 'I'm not sure about sex but it looks a bit foreign to me.' She was silent for a while, struggling with her conscience. 'Do you know, I don't think I can resist using that ticket.'

'You're free on Friday, then? By the way, if Frank can't or won't go with you, don't ask me. He used to be a good friend of mine. You can enjoy the concert with a perfectly clear conscience you know: I'm quite sure Linda wouldn't want to go.'

'You know her fairly well then?'

He nodded. 'I visited fairly often. Graham was quite proud of Linda, liked to show her off. She's got a flair for clothes, she's quick witted, and a good housekeeper, everything spick and span. I made myself agreeable for his sake.'

'What does she do?'

'To earn a living? Not a lot. She taught till Peter was born, stayed at home until he was old enough for school, then did bits of supply teaching and coaching on and off till she became pregnant again. She was really tied once Helena arrived, of course, and I must admit she's a good mother to her. Keeps her spick and span too, which isn't easy. She's still in nappies all day at going on four.'

Zoe realized he was trying to override his dislike and give an unbiased assessment. 'I think they'd have had a better marriage if

112

Linda had gone on working, at least after Peter went to school. Then she could have been more independent of Graham and wouldn't have expected him to fulfil all her ambitions for her.'

Zoe nodded. 'You're probably right. You couldn't get hold of a photograph of him, could you? If I knew what he looked like I'd feel I knew him better. At the moment, he's just a figment of my imagination. You can tell a lot about people from their faces.'

Cameron looked sceptical, but was prepared to humour her. 'I've got all the pictures taken at the club annual dinner in the car. I'll trade a trip out in the filthy fog for another cup of your excellent coffee.'

Zoe looked conscience-stricken. 'That's the second time you've had to prompt me to offer you a basic courtesy. Will it compensate you if I invite you to lunch?'

He grinned. 'It would, but I won't accept, if you don't mind. There's always the possibility that Frank might call in to eat with you and goodness knows what he'd read into finding us at the same table.'

Zoe swivelled the chair and disappeared into the kitchen. She heard the muffled slamming of the car door through the slightly opened window as she bustled about. When she carried the tray back to the sitting-room, the wallet of postcard-sized snapshots was lying on the coffee-table.

She left Cameron to dispense the coffee and looked through them thoughtfully. He hovered. 'I'll show you...' But Zoe shook her head. She reached for the tray, now empty, and began to lay the pictures out on it, studying the various groups as they ate, talked and danced.

It was not difficult to pick out Graham Crowther. Age and sex eliminated a good many of the subjects and Cameron nodded an affirmative as she pointed to a slight, grey-blond figure, who smiled ingratiatingly at the photographer. The face was thin with a broad forehead. Zoe thought the hair was not receding but had probably always grown like that, in a straight line high across the brow. The hair was a little too long to go with the formal clothes, which the man wore uncomfortably, almost as if they were borrowed.

Zoe closed her eyes for several seconds, then looked at the picture again. Was the man really smiling so sycophantically, or was she reading into his face the impressions that Cameron had fed her? She studied the features, looking for the opposite characteristics. She couldn't find them there.

Nodding to acknowledge the full cup that Cameron pushed towards her, Zoe picked up two of the pictures. 'Can I borrow these?' She would come fresh to them later on and see what they suggested to her away from Cameron's influence. After all, their opinions of Linda Crowther were not identical. Zoe's first impression had been unfavourable but her sympathy had grown as she understood, increasingly, how and why the woman had become as she was.

'It will be interesting,' she found herself saying, 'to hear what his building-society colleagues and family have to say about him at the funeral this afternoon.'

Zoe knew at once that the remark was a mistake. Cameron put down his cup and stared at her. 'You'll be there? How come?' His thought processes clicked on inevitably. 'You know her. Why didn't you say? You see her in secret at that Relate place!' It had been a stab in the dark but she knew her face had confirmed it. His tone became accusing. 'You're on her side!' He looked like Adonis and sounded like a child in an infant-school playground.

Zoe sighed. 'I'm interested in making sure that Graham wasn't a victim of—well, murder, I suppose. I'm not interested in your vendetta against his wife. If you've finished that coffee, I think you'd better go. I'll see you at the funeral.'

Peter Crowther looked up as his girl-friend came into the sitting room. 'Where's your mother?' she demanded.

'What do you want her for?'

The girl shrugged. 'Only to ask if there's anything I can do, but I can't find her.' She wandered over to the window and glared out at wizened and barely discernible rose-bushes badly in need of pruning.

'She's gone to the restaurant that's doing the "funeral meats",' Peter volunteered. 'We were going to have the guests back here at the house but on Friday Mum invited a woman in a wheelchair. She spent Saturday frantically trying to find a place that a wheelchair can get into and that could lay on something at such short notice. Now she's gone to check over their arrangements.'

'Some relative she'd forgotten?'

Peter shook his head. 'No, it's apparently someone she's only just met. Says she's a wonderful moral support.' He waved his hands to indicate his mother's unaccount-ability. 'She was always a law unto herself.'

Rachel turned back to the window. 'Is it all right for Helena to be outside? It's a bit cold and damp...'

116

'Hell, no!' His book fell to the floor as he leaped to his feet. 'I'm supposed to be looking after her. She catches cold easily, then she gets serious breathing problems.'

Rachel was out before him, gathering the child into her arms until halted by ear-splitting shrieks and a painful kick. She watched, shivering, as Peter spent five patient minutes coaxing his sister inside.

'If you come in quietly with me,' he promised, suddenly inspired, 'I'll find you your dangle.'

'What's that?' Rachel spoke in a whisper, fearful of further upsetting the now angelically smiling child.

Peter answered by holding it up, a bright plastic ball threaded on to what looked like an old dressing-gown cord. He hung it on a small hook on the wall and set it swinging. Helena sat quietly on the floor, mesmerized by the movement. 'Mum hates her playing with this, but it's harmless. It means we can have the telly off and it stops her thinking about food. She loves eating and you can see she puts on weight easily. Talking of food, do you fancy a coffee? She'll be happy there now for a while but just watch her till I come back.'

As he set out cups, he could hear Rachel using her 'jolly' voice to address his sister loudly, as though she were deaf. Still, Helena had been a bit of a shock to

Rachel and she was doing her best. He felt mean for bringing her here. Mum was at her most difficult and in any case a funeral wasn't an easy occasion to get to know your boy-friend's family better. At least after the first few seconds she had managed not to stare at Helena's lolling tongue and peculiar staggering walk.

His sister's real problems were not so much within the family but with the lack of understanding of the 'normal' community. Helena wasn't handicapped within the scope of her own existence. She was as she was. She was found wanting only in relation to the kind of demands made by the society in which she had to live. Dad had helped him to understand that, though he had never got it across to Mum.

Most of the time, Mum seemed to think that Helena's condition was just another of Dad's failures. Dad was never apologetic about her, he just plodded wearily on with all the drudgery that looking after her entailed. Peter wondered why she'd been conceived. Obviously, his parents hadn't intended to have a Down's child but they must have known the risks. She was more likely just an accident than a last fling. Mum didn't have flings; she was too buttoned-up. He'd thought they were well past all that. Not biologically, of course, but they were hardly dream lovers any more—if they ever had been.

He remembered his father's first explanation to him of the facts of life. At ten, Peter had simply refused to believe him. He still found it difficult to accept that his mother had connived in such an activity to produce himself. For a while he had enjoyed lively fantasies about how his father had achieved copulation, by force or by trickery. With increased maturity he had decided the fantasies were probably not too far removed from the truth.

He wondered if his father had had a mistress. He hoped so. He rather liked the idea of him being willingly received by somebody, but thought it unlikely. He shook his head to clear it and carried the tray into the sitting-room. Helena was safely dangling still and Rachel dutifully watching her.

Peter approached his sister and attempted to insert the spout of her baby-cup between her lips. She spat it out and knocked the cup out of his hand. Rachel fetched a cloth and mopped. Peter drank coffee and continued to think about his parents. He knew that what his mother found hardest to take about Helena was that she was a 'touching' child. She had tempers and tantrums but in a good mood she would stroke people as she smiled at them. Mum couldn't bear it. Gran, on the other hand, had come round to her because of these displays of affection.

Half the time Peter felt fiercely indignant on his father's behalf, and the rest he had felt impatient with him. He couldn't have envisaged a scene where his father turned on his mother. It hadn't been in him. It had never occurred to him that he didn't need to listen to her twisted arguments and get involved in her clever word-play, that he could just have walked away from it. Sometimes he'd appeared to do that, but he'd never been able to resist showing her she'd wounded him—in the tone of his voice or the slam of the door.

Not that Mum was victorious, either, in the long run. She won the argument but she didn't get him to do what she wanted. She didn't get her own way.

Peter's eyes followed the swing of his sister's bauble until he became unaware of both her and Rachel. He'd been able to tell from his questions that at least one of the policemen who had called suspected that his father had committed suicide. In a way, it would have been typical of Dad. In some moods he might have done it. Rob Cameron thought not, but Peter thought he might have considered it if he had been desperate enough. Would he really have gone through with it?

Mum's account was odd, didn't feel right. Did Dad really write a note? It was funny that it hadn't turned up in the waste-bin. There weren't any open fires to burn it on. It was funny, too, that Dad had decided to sleep in the spare room. That was more Mum's sort of trick, melodramatic gestures.

And it was laughable to think he had tidied away his bedclothes and breakfast dishes, almost as laughable as the idea of his going off for a session on the river without any breakfast. He was more likely to have made a nice calculation of the calories he had taken in balanced against the energy he was likely to expend.

'You're not saying much,' Rachel remarked, plaintively.

He smiled at her. 'I'm really grateful to you, Rache. I know it's uncomfortable for you here. You hardly knew my father and you don't know where you are with my mum, and Helena embarrasses you, but I need you here. You're sane and normal.'

She came to sit beside him and he took her hand. 'Have you ever met my father except when you've been with me?'

She stared at him. 'What a weird question. I wouldn't have known who he was till last Easter when your parents came to see you at college. I've only seen him twice since then, when he picked you

121

up from our house in the summer and when he drove you back to college at the beginning of this term.'

'I know. Forget it.'

He blessed Helena for setting up a caterwauling that distracted Rachel. It didn't seem likely that any kind of relationship had developed between her and his father not even in his father's vivid imagination, on those few occasions. Anyway, the rumour had reached him by a very circuitous route. Spensely had been quite a drinker, even when they were both in the fourth form. By now, he probably had delusions and what he thought he had overheard between Dad and Rob Cameron at the canoe-club dinner could safely be forgotten. Besides, who'd have looked at Dad twice, even among women his own age?

Chapter Eight

A wind had arisen during the late morning and removed the choking fog, together with all the remaining leaves from the trees in the grounds of the crematorium. Zoe was reminded of the desolation of Twelfth-night, when her mother insisted that every vestige of Christmas gaiety must be laid away until next year. Branches were stark against an ice-blue sky and isolated snowflakes meandered down between gusts.

In addition to putting on winter boots and woollen trousers, she had reluctantly draped her knees with a substantial rug. Bitter experience had taught her to respect her sluggish circulation since she could not join in the various slappings and stampings being indulged in by the rest of the assembled company. She bore the old-lady image with ill-grace.

She had parted on bad terms with Rob Cameron but she was glad of his arrival now, as a distraction from the covert glances of the other guests. Why, for goodness' sake, could they not include her in the subdued conversation? They were all from disparate groups, strangers to each other, having only their connection with Graham Crowther in common, yet they all exchanged polite pleasantries with each other. It could only be the wheelchair that excluded her.

Cameron's manner was easy. He introduced Zoe to several canoeists whose faces she recognized from the previous Thursday and she filed away their names.

The gathering focused now on the arrival of the family limousines as the first one drew up, smooth and black. Linda Crowther climbed out, followed by a boy, presumably Peter, and a girl of roughly the same age. It took the efforts of all three and the driver to extricate two distressed old ladies.

Zoe regarded Peter curiously. He was tall and slight with his father's broad brow and bony features. His rather lank hair was tied back from his face with what appeared to be a black bootlace, but he was otherwise smartly dressed in dark garments. The girl seemed to have draped herself with any items of clothing she could find that were sufficiently subdued, everything mismatched, but the effect was overridden by her youth and wholesomeness. 'Pete's girlfriend,' Cameron hissed in Zoe's ear.

The group slowly approached the crematorium entrance, Peter walking beside his mother and the girl behind, smilingly offering each of the decrepit ladies an arm. The second car disgorged a further collection of assorted relatives. The shivering remainder brought up the rear.

Zoe had done her homework. The door with the ramp was at the front of the chapel. She slipped through and rolled up the side aisle as the rest of the company entered from the back and cast off from the centre aisle. Unbidden, Cameron walked easily beside the chair, falling behind as they entered the building. When Zoe parked at the back, the hindmost row of guests, assuming they were a pair, moved up and made room for Cameron.

There seemed to be no service books, but an official distributed sheets on which the Twenty-Third Psalm was set to the tune Crimond. Zoe lifted her clear strong soprano with enthusiasm until she realized heads were turning. The volume had to be reduced for 'In death's dark vale' anyway, and she kept the remainder pianissimo as she looked round. The coffin and window sills held white lilies. Graham Crowther had not struck her as a lily sort of man, but she supposed the arrangements were not for his benefit.

The proceedings were unremarkable except for the eulogy. Zoe was unsure of the status of the speaker but felt that

125

he had neither known the deceased well himself, nor been briefed by anyone who did. It was the epitome of a eulogy. Graham had possessed all the general virtues but, apparently, no particular one, except his prowess at watersports, which produced sheepish grins along two rows, hastily concealed and controlled.

Later, at the restaurant, the usual post-funeral atmosphere prevailed, the reassertion of a guilty cheerfulness, justified by a continuation of the eulogy and the trite and convenient conclusion that life has to go on. Zoe was content, warm and about, she hoped, to be fed comestibles and information.

Cameron had arrived at the crematorium on foot, having failed to resurrect a dead car-battery. Zoe had felt obliged to offer him a lift but had dismissed him as soon as they reached the restaurant car-park. She glared at him as he showed signs of helping to unload her chair. 'Keep out of my hair,' she warned him. 'I'm going to circulate alone, announcing that I'm Linda's friend who has never met Graham. Let's see what they'll tell me.'

They told a good deal. Zoe quickly learned that Graham had played a mean game of chess, had been a twin whose brother had died in infancy; had been captain of the grammar school's swimming team. As the wine flowed, various informants shared their opinions that Peter was a spoilt brat too proud to get his hands dirty, that Linda had married beneath her and that the Crowther family should be sued because the leaking gutter that Graham had failed to repair had ruined the decorations in his neighbour's bedroom.

Towards the end of the proceedings, Zoe engaged in conversation with an ancient uncle who sat in a corner, keeping a hiccupping tryst with an empty whisky bottle. He showed a strong inclination to climb into the wheelchair with her as he confided that he'd always predicted a sticky end for young Gray, who had been a 'lying little toad' ever since he could talk. 'Tales he expected me to believe! Must o' thought I was a tile short. Anything to make himself look big—and all so pointless. I could have understood it if it had been to get himself out o' trouble. That's only kid-like.'

Having ascertained that the old man was not driving, Zoe bought him another double and settled down to encourage him. After only a few minutes she had decided that, if the deceased had been a pathological liar, then she could guess from which of his forebears he had inherited the gene for it.

Across the room, Cameron had made

several mimed offers of rescue which Zoe had refused with a frown. Now, she grinned at him and he stepped over smartly. 'This is Robert, one of Graham's canoeing friends,' she told the old man. 'I'm sure he'd be interested in what you've been telling me.' She smiled sweetly at Cameron as she swung away. That would teach him!

The reckoning came fifteen minutes later, after Cameron had been obliged to assist the uncle's minder to pack him into a taxi. He was not pleased and enumerated his grudges against Zoe in an undertone. 'It's senseless not to accept help that gets you indoors more quickly on a freezing day.' So, he had wanted to set up the chair for her. 'And we shan't get many more opportunities like today. We need to find out all we can, not play silly jokes on each other.'

'I thought we'd come to pay our last respects—you, anyway.' He blushed. 'You're right, though, and I owe you a drink.' He brightened. 'However, as you say, we mustn't waste this opportunity. We need our wits about us. I'll buy you some orange juice.'

The bar was crowded by now, but Zoe, having used her usual technique, was back in short order. They drank and shared information, Cameron hearing Zoe out first. 'Nothing terribly useful,' she summarized, 'but interesting. By the way, Linda introduced me, both to her doctor and to Helena's health visitor, as "the lady from Relate who's been trying to help me sort my marriage out". It makes me feel less guilty about you finding out that I'm counselling her, but I wonder why she wanted people to know. She not only said who I was but she made a point of my meeting them. Why? And she made no attempt to lower her voice or draw us aside.'

Linda approached the pair now as they chatted together. She was beautifully made up and her hair was newly tinted. The silver-grey suit jacket skimmed her padded midriff as kindly as the leather jacket had done. She addressed Cameron. 'Where's Frank? I haven't seen him.'

'It's his ops day. He can't get away if the list's long or if he's worried about a post-operative animal. He only said he might get here.' Linda looked surprised to get her answer from Zoe and moved away as Peter called her.

Cameron asked, 'What did you talk about to these medical people?'

'I asked the doc how wise it was for angina patients to do canoeing and what he felt about advising people whose favourite pursuits were bad for them. He didn't seem to think it was a problem. He had his patient sussed and knew he didn't exert himself very much. He thought the sudden effort he'd made on Sunday morning had been unaccustomed and had exhausted him so that he couldn't swim properly. He did swim well, didn't he?'

Cameron was laconic. 'Not after hitting his head on a branch, or having it done for him. I've been talking to Ken Hammond, the chap who found the body and saw the mysterious angler. I got him to go over it all again. He fishes himself. He didn't get a very clear view of whoever it was. He was busy attending to his lad and wondering what to do about Graham. He said it was a smallish man, could have been a tall woman. He couldn't tell by the walk because the figure was muffled up and laden. He did notice that whoever it was carried a top-of-the-range Hardy rod. He says one day he's going to sell his house to buy one for himself. One odd thing—the clothes appeared to be wet and it was a lovely bright morning. Ken wasn't out till about nine, though. The fisherman could have been there since the early hours.

'I talked to some of the building-society types. Boring lot. There doesn't seem to be much truth in the stories Graham circulated about his being God's gift to accountancy. They used non-commital phrases like "steady", "loyal", "always ready to help less experienced people".'

They sipped fruit juice and tried to look as though they were enjoying it. 'I managed one useful thing,' Zoe volunteered after a minute. 'I rearranged Linda's appointment at Relate for Thursday instead of Friday. Now I'm free for my jaunt to the Festival Hall.'

Cameron drained his glass. 'I didn't realize until this morning what brilliant opportunities you were getting to hear the inside info on the Crowthers. We'll have to have another consultation before Thursday to think up some leading questions.'

Zoe swung her chair away from him. 'I'm going now. I'll pretend I didn't hear that.'

A figure got up and opened the door for her, then hurried ahead to repeat the courtesy at the one that led outside. Zoe bit her lip firmly. Today's youth was proving it could be well mannered. She smiled at Peter encouragingly as he hesitated beside her: 'Can I help you?'

'Well, maybe I've found out why you're here.' Zoe blinked. 'Sorry. I meant I realize now what your connection is with my mother. I was wondering if you talked to sons too.'

Zoe grinned. 'Having girl-friend trouble?'

He shook his head. 'Definitely not.' He shuffled his feet.

'It's about your mother then.'

'That's right. Can I make an appointment?'

'You could, but why don't you come to the house? That would get round having to put you on the waiting list.' He smiled. 'Tomorrow? Half-ten?' She scribbled the address on a scrap of paper from her bag. He thanked her and turned to go back, but hesitantly. 'Was there something else?'

'It will still be confidential—if it's at your house—won't it?'

Zoe reassured him. She wondered whether Linda would have been so keen for her to attend the funeral if she could have anticipated this request from her son.

Zoe's first two priorities when she arrived home were to get warm and to set some music playing. When she had first come out of hospital, she had heard people say that her music would be a great solace to her, as though it were a second-best occupation, a compensation for what she had lost and would rather have.

In fact, singing, both active and passive, gave her her keenest pleasure. Now, the impossibility of more practically useful pursuits, her career, for example, had given her the time to explore it properly and find a delight that almost wounded her with its intensity. She reached first for the Schubert symphony she had failed to recognize on the radio recently, but pushed it back after a moment in favour of a collection of Bruckner motets.

She had always sung but never played an instrument since an aborted series of piano lessons as a very small child. During the long, bedridden weeks when she had thought she might never work again, she had thought she might give it another go, on something a little more portable. She still had half an intention of trying the flute but she couldn't find the time to get started. She found plenty of time for singing, so maybe she had no real desire to play.

She slipped the Bruckner into the machine. The choir on the disc began to sing. 'Os justi' was not Zoe's favourite. She spent most of the five minutes and seven seconds of it fidgeting and chafing her hands. Then, warmed and comfortable, she sat perfectly still, giving her whole attention to 'Locus iste'.

Irreprehensibilis est,' whispered round the room, the vowels dwelt on and the sibilants skilfully subdued. What a little gem. Two minutes and forty-one seconds of bliss; but now Zoe had to give thought to preparing a meal. Tonight was choir practice and Frank would arrive, depressed or elated according to how his ops had gone, but in good time for her to report for duty.

If things were right between them, he would do the washing-up: Monday-evening help had nothing to do with her disability. She wouldn't *ask* him to do it, though. That deviation from the norm would acknowledge the tension between them, the doldrums through which their relationship was passing. Well, she hoped it was passing.

'*Libera me, Domine!*' Zoe joined in the first delicious, soaring intercession of the next motet as she began to chop bacon.

By the coffee break, midway through her rehearsal, Zoe had sung herself into a euphoric optimism. After their meal, Frank had cleared the table without comment and immersed the greasy dishes in hot suds. He would soon realize he was being stupid to resent her easy relationship with Rob Cameron. Besides, now Linda had let it be known that she was a Relate client, she could explain, at least in part, why she had agreed to look into Cameron's suspicions and, therefore, why she kept seeing him. Besides, by this time on Friday, she and Frank would be listening to Jeffie Lister in the Festival Hall.

She shared this latter good news with a fellow-soprano, who expressed a gratifying envy and volunteered the information that her aged neighbour was Jeffie's great-aunt. The second half of the rehearsal was less of a romp. Their earlier frolic through part one of Dvořák's 'Stabat Mater' had been found wanting. Zoe forgot Frank and the Festival Hall and the Crowthers as she applied herself to putting it right.

When she eventually arrived home, she was intrigued to see that Frank's car was still outside her house.

When her telephone rang just before ten o'clock on Tuesday morning, Zoe was rather disappointed: so, Peter Crowther had changed his mind. But the voice that was speaking to her was definitely that of an elderly lady.

Her name, she announced, was Mary Lister. That would mean nothing to Zoe of course. She *would* recognize the name of Margaret Jessop, of course, and Zoe would have heard of *Jennifer* Lister, of course.

'Of course,' Zoe assured her, before she could stop herself. 'Would you be Jeffie's aunt? Margaret mentioned you last night.'

'*Great*-aunt,' the voice corrected, half hurt, half offended.

'Sorry.' Zoe had meant the omission to be tactful. 'Is there something I can do for you?' Please God, not another investigation.

135

It turned out to be merely the delivery of a necklace that Jennifer particularly wished to wear at a concert in a fortnight's time. 'It will *belong* to her eventually, of course, and I was wondering how I could get it to her. I could hardly send such a valuable thing through the post, of course.'

'Naturally not.' This time Zoe had her tongue under better control. With difficulty, she persuaded the old lady to give the address of her house and instructions for reaching it. Too late, it occurred to her that she could have obtained this information from Margaret. Perhaps she would check with her anyway.

Her visitor eventually arrived, so late that Zoe had decided once again that he had changed his mind. He refused to remove his coat and hovered in the hall as though undecided whether to stay. When she offered coffee, ready filtered and waiting to be poured, he refused that too.

'I don't mean to be rude,' he assured her. 'It's just that Mum wanted me to mind Helena again this morning and the shopping I'd planned as my excuse for being out seemed a movable feast. Mum doesn't give books for my course a high priority since I refused to consider doing computing or science, where she thinks there's money and fame to be had.'

'What are you studying?'

'English. Mum says it'll get me nowhere and that I'm a loser like Dad.' Zoe was appalled but not surprised. 'She said if I must stay on the arts side, why not PPE or history. That way I might get into government at some level.' And this mother had assured Zoe that she had avoided the mistakes of her own upbringing and given her son freedom to choose.

'So, how did you manage to get here?'

A smile transformed his face. 'As usual, Rachel stepped in. She's coping with Helena on her own, that's why I mustn't be long. Rachel might not have been so keen to help if she'd known what Mum was up to.'

'What do you mean?' Zoe was intrigued. Whilst she still had the impression that Linda had presented herself at Relate for other reasons than to try to save a failing marriage, she could have sworn that her client's revelations about her sexual inhibitions were perfectly genuine. Was Peter now suggesting that his mother was involved with another man?

He was not. 'She's going round the shops in town, stealing from them, unless I'm very much mistaken.' Zoe was surprised and yet found herself quite able to believe him. 'It's the only explanation for the situation at home. I know there's no

137

money to spare, but we're not at all short of the things Mum wants and values. Dad suspected ages ago and sounded me out about it indirectly, then we began collecting evidence. I don't think I'm the only one who suspects either. I think that's the reason Mum and Helena were assigned a social worker this week.'

'Don't you think having a handicapped child and suddenly losing her husband would account for it?'

He stared at her for a long moment, as though she had let him down. 'For the social worker or the stealing? I don't know. She never seemed to have much time for Dad. When he was sure she was taking things he threatened to expose her unless she...well, came up with the goods in bed. It didn't work. She told him he'd be playing right into her hands, whatever that was supposed to mean. Maybe you know more about the state of things between them than I do. She says you understand her.'

Did she? Zoe wondered. 'I suppose she means I don't condemn her. How do you know about this moral blackmail of your father's?'

'They argued in piercing undertones and they thought if my nose was in a book then I was deaf. Besides, he did it a lot. He did it to Rob.' Zoe's heart sank as she anticipated what was coming. 'Rob got into trouble a few years ago for taking performance-enhancing drugs. Dad found out and he and Rob have had a bosom friendship ever since.'

'And how much of that is pure speculation?'

The boy shrugged. 'I believe it. There are plenty of drugs available round here. You don't need telling that, and I know because I've been offered them. I don't suppose it was different five years or so ago. Rob wouldn't be his friend in the normal course of things. He doesn't suffer fools gladly, especially when they hamper him in his work.'

'That's a harsh way to talk about your father.'

The boy nodded soberly. 'I know. Dad had a hell of a life. I loved him but I didn't respect him. I wouldn't talk about him like this to anyone else. It's just that my mother's been very frank with you about the things she wants you to know. You can do your job better if you know the rest. Rob's told me about you.'

This was cryptic. 'What about me?'

'Your accident. Your police work.'

'Are you interested in joining the police?'

He shrugged. 'I don't know. I might be.' He sat plaiting his fingers until she helped him out.

'Is this what you came to tell me? If not, then I suggest you come straight out with what you want to say. I don't want to rush you but it's not me who's in a hurry.'

He looked mightily relieved at the direct approach. 'Right. Rachel and I went up to Keele at the same time and we've been seeing each other for eighteen months now. I like her a lot. I've heard rumours about her and Dad, varying ones. Someone told me she was upset because he'd been annoying her with his attentions, wouldn't leave her alone. Then someone wrote to me to say they'd had weekends together when Mum thought Dad was canoeing. I don't know whether you ever had a counselling session with Dad but I need to find out what was going on, if there was anything.'

'What does Rachel say? Doesn't she spend her weekends with you?'

He nodded. 'Most of them, but...'

'Why don't you ask her?'

He looked aghast. 'Whatever would she think if I'm wrong? And I'm sure I am, but...I can't get it out of my head.'

'Would you believe her if she denied it?'

He answered with no hesitation. 'Yes, yes I would.'

'Does she behave as though she had a

140

guilty secret?' He shook his head. 'You accept her word but you think she might act out a lie?'

'No, of course not, but she might have been bothered by him and not told me.'

'Couldn't you ask her that?'

He smiled. 'Yes, I could ask her if I put it like that. Why couldn't I work that out for myself?'

'You just needed to be away from all your other distractions.'

'Your house is very peaceful. Could I have that coffee after all?' Zoe propelled the chair to the coffee machine, noting that Peter, maybe warned by Rob Cameron, made no attempt to assist her.

'There's something else?'

'Well, just that I feel guilty leaving Mum on her own. Will she cope with Helena?'

Zoe was asking herself the same question. 'She took it on herself. She could have had her aborted or adopted.'

He sniffed. 'Not without offending the matriarchs—my grans. It's the only thing the two of them have ever agreed about. Grandma Kelsey said all the same things as those pro-life people and Grannie Crowther said These Little Ones are sent with a Purpose. Saying that seemed to me to devalue Helena's existence as much as doing away with her would have done.' He changed his mind again as Zoe reached to pour his coffee. 'I can't. I'll have to go. Rachel might not be wise to all Helena's tricks.'

Zoe put the jug down again. 'Before you go, are you willing to tell me who offered you drugs?'

He smiled. 'A schoolmate, whose name I won't give you. He got them from his father who got them from a respected councillor—but I doubt you'll ever catch him at it or get anybody to testify against him.' He handed Zoe a scrap of paper from his wallet. 'This is my address and telephone number in Keele. Please get in touch with me if Mum gets into any trouble with the police.'

Chapter Nine

Peter had correctly guessed his mother's morning occupation. Back in Molloy's, wearing the silver-grey funeral suit with a crisp white blouse, as yesterday. Now, she decided, she needed something to cheer it up for a happier occasion.

The suit was of such excellent quality that she could not bear to spoil the effect with inferior accessories. She had rejected conventional pink and gone for sharp yellow. Later in the season, a touch of green would make it an ideal spring outfit. She had consulted a complete stranger to advise on the yellow blouse. 'I know it goes well with the grey, but does it make me look sallow?'

The fellow-shopper had been most helpful. 'It looks wonderful, but for a change, you could just button the jacket right up and wear some antique silver, a heavy link necklace and drop ear-rings.' What a good idea. Not the real thing, of course: that was too well guarded, but there was a costume-jewellery shop in the precinct, called Jingles, where the shop floor was filled with stylized

143

wooden trees, the branches hung with all of its wares. She had seen some perfectly acceptable reproduction stuff there, but she might as well investigate the jewellery department here to get some idea of what she wanted.

As she browsed, Linda noticed her helpful friend again, and yet again later, in shoes and hosiery. It occurred to her that the woman just might be the store detective. Of course, her whole idea was to have a day of reckoning in the not too distant future, but she had not had this particular day in mind, not when Peter and Rachel were at home to witness her humiliation.

She smiled and waved nonchalantly, remembering that the woman had casually asked whether she had got her suit at Molloy's. What a fool she had been to admit it. It was a new line and Molloy's, though an old-established shop, was only a small business in a smallish town. They would only have ordered a few copies of the model and the staff would know that none of them had sold the missing one.

A well-bred, penetrating voice distracted Linda from her worries. '*So* pleased to see you're bearing up so well...such a very pleasant, helpful man always...your kind hospitality of yesterday...*do* let me buy you some coffee this morning.'

Georgina Groves, married to a bigwig from Graham's firm and their only posh neighbour. For several years Linda had worked hard to be accepted as a visitor in her house. It was a pity that Graham's pleasantness and helpfulness, so generously acknowledged verbally, had not been equally readily recognized in his pay cheques and promotions.

Linda smiled as she was swept into the restaurant—the waitress-service one this time. Maybe she had fathomed a way of obtaining free refreshments after all. Soon she was happily contemplating Georgina's tiers of chins from behind a plate of buttered scones.

The commiserations continued and Linda felt slightly self-conscious as she propped her bulging carrier-bags against the table-leg. It hadn't occurred to her before, but maybe Georgina would think it a little odd to find her out on a spending spree on the morning after her husband's funeral. 'I'm trying not to sit about moping,' she justified herself. 'It wouldn't be good for Helena. And people will still expect Christmas presents. I'm putting a few together whilst Peter and Rachel are still at home to mind her for me.'

Looking up, she caught the eye of the woman who had been following her. She had just entered the restaurant and now sat at a table by the door. She'd followed her here too! Linda's throat closed against a clogged mass of chewed scone. They didn't challenge you until you'd actually left the store with the goods on your person. How could she prevent the punctiliously polite Georgina from escorting her all the way back to her car with her parcels?

The woman, she noticed, had taken a notebook from her handbag and was jotting in it. Georgina, intent on her own hearty encouragement, was oblivious of Linda's silence. What a fool she'd been, not to choose somewhere miles from home to work this racket.

Suddenly, she leaped to her feet, praying that she would reach the cloakroom. By the time Georgina had lumbered after her, she was swirling water vigorously round the sink and wiping her eyes and mouth.

Georgina twittered. 'You poor dear. Are you all right now? Come and sit down and see if you can sip some tea.' When they returned to their table to order a fresh pot, the woman had disappeared from her spot near the entrance. So had all Linda's 'shopping' and Georgina's handbag.

Zoe was glad to hear Benny Mitchell's voice when she picked up the telephone receiver. 'There's no startling news but

I'm only two streets away and due to go off duty.'

Zoe supplied the required invitation, then, as she waited, tried to impose order on the turbulent facts, ideas and suspicions coursing through her head. How could she possibly judge whether or not a man she had never met might have committed suicide; or driven his wife, or some other person, to drown him; or drowned, in an accident caused by his own negligence, when strict adherence to safety procedures was, according to his friends and acquaintances, part of his religion?

'A few weeks in CID and you'd soon have all that sorted out,' DC Mitchell told her when she expressed her frustrating lack of familiarity with the people she had been called upon to judge. 'Facing the questions, I mean, not finding the answers. When we start a murder investigation, we don't usually have any personal knowledge of the victim. Getting to know him is the first task, and it makes all the others easier.'

Zoe nodded. 'How's Ginny, by the way? I'm forgetting my manners.'

Mitchell grinned. 'In her usual state at three months' gestation. Have bucket, will travel.'

Zoe laughed. 'Don't be vulgar, and

don't joke about it. She won't think it's funny!'

'Joke? I daren't even mention it. She copes by totally ignoring it and I have to too. It's quite difficult, especially when I'm responsible.'

'Only half responsible, surely. To get back to the Crowthers, Rob has just about convinced me that Graham is not likely to have killed himself. Apart from his shrinking from physical danger, there doesn't seem to have been anything recently to make his life suddenly more unbearable. Why are we both unhappy with the misadventure verdict? Why can't we accept that it was a simple accident?' Zoe wound long strands of hair round her fingers as she sought an answer. The activity produced only another question. 'Why hasn't the angler come forward?'

Mitchell was dismissive. 'Plenty of reasons. He's gone abroad. He's no friend of the fuzz. Almost certainly, he doesn't like canoeists—fishermen are always arguing with them about their irreconcilable rights on the water. Maybe he was up to some other mischief that he wants to keep quiet, nothing to do with Graham.'

Zoe contributed a reason of her own. 'Maybe he was a visitor, not local. The drowning has only been reported in the

148

Clarion. He might not know you'd like to talk to him.' She added, after a pause, 'I think Rob's idea is that Linda was the muffled angler. It wasn't a bad morning. He thinks the scarves and things were a disguise.'

'Is that your idea too?'

Zoe's restless fingers embroiled the lock of hair with a button. She freed it impatiently. 'Linda's a conundrum. I began by thinking that someone who talked about herself so much was unlikely to take any positive action, least of all something as drastic as killing someone. I still think it's true on the whole, but I wouldn't rule out a desperate, impulsive action in an emergency.'

'Dressing up as a fisherman to wade into a river and drown your husband sounds more deliberately vindictive than impulsive. I understand that she wasn't madly in love with her husband, but I can't see that she would have had much to gain by killing him. And I certainly can't see why anyone else would want to. To the rest of mankind he seems to have been a temporary and minor irritation. And where would Linda Crowther have got a Hardy rod from?'

Zoe's fingers were already tangling her hair with the button again. 'Which of those do you want me to consider first? While I

149

was waiting for you, I was wondering if the boy had anything to do with it. He's been to see me.'

'Wasn't he at Keele?'

'He was supposed to be but no one's checked.' She saw his face change and followed his gaze to see Rob Cameron's car drawing up outside. When she let him in, the two men nodded curtly to each other. Ignoring their obvious animosity, she described Peter's visit, omitting, for reasons she refused to acknowledge to herself, his accusations against Cameron and his theories about the friendship between Cameron and his father.

They listened in a silence which continued as each of them tried to assess the importance and the truth of the information the boy had volunteered. Finally, the two men spoke simultaneously.

Cameron desisted and Mitchell asked. 'You think he might have got rid of his father to get his woman back?'

Zoe shook her head. 'Not really. He can probably prove he was safely in Keele. No! Forget that, he probably can't, not at that hour on a Sunday morning. What were you going to say, Rob?'

'Graham put the story about himself. His version was that Rachel had a crush on him right from their first meeting when he and Linda visited Peter at Keele. The

150

club version was the exact opposite, that he took a fancy to his son's girl-friend and made a play for her on and off ever since. The whole story got well exaggerated in the pub a while ago.'

'So, what really happened?' Mitchell demanded.

'Precisely nothing, I'd say. So that probably convinces you that there was a red-hot affair going on...'

'But it's what *Peter* thought that's important.' Zoe glanced at Mitchell. 'Is it possible to make tactful enquiries at his university without actually asking him where he was? If I'd had my wits about me this morning, I might have got him to tell me in the course of ordinary conversation whether he was or was not innocently in his bed.'

'Maybe we could ask Rachel. With a bit of luck, she might have been in it with him.'

Zoe considered Cameron's suggestion but shook her head. 'There isn't a police investigation going on. We can't just wade in and cross-question everybody as though they're suspects when officially no crime has been committed.'

'What about the shop-lifting story?'

Cameron shrugged. 'I thought spending every penny he earned on putting expensive clothes on her back was just another example of Graham's weak character, giving her what she wanted to shut her up. Maybe he didn't. Hello, you've got another visitor.' He turned back from the window. 'It's only Frank.'

Zoe sighed. Only Frank! Now this bizarre Tuesday-morning party would become even more difficult to manage. She would not, she decided, offer them coffee. The easiest way to cope was to get rid of at least some of them. There were as many questions circulating in her mind about the various relationships between the four of them as about the Crowthers.

When Frank caught sight of Cameron, he looked angry. When Benny too stepped forward his expression became puzzled. She thought it was the half-embarrassed silence that led him to demand, 'What's going on?' Zoe was irritated. It was her house. She could invite into it whomever she chose. Nevertheless, he had, she decided, the right to be put in the picture at least as fully as the other two. She wondered where to begin.

Benny, it seemed, had been thinking along the same lines. To save more of her hair falling foul of her jacket-buttons, he helped out. 'You know that Graham Crowther drowned last Sunday morning?' Frank listened without interruption until the detective constable had finished.

'So, your superintendent found no reason to suspect foul play, but several officers, including yourself, were unhappy when it was decided not to investigate the death?'

Zoe nodded. 'And Rob was equally unhappy and approached me.'

Cameron added defensively, 'I'd discovered she was an ex-police constable. I wanted to know if anything could be done.'

Suddenly, Frank smiled. 'I came to cadge an early lunch. Can I potter round the kitchen whilst you folk carry on? I'll make coffee if you like.'

Zoe and Mitchell exchanged winks. His coffee was only marginally better than Ginny's, but under the circumstances they would happily drink it. They settled down again, leaving the door open so that Frank could hear.

'What about the rod?' Zoe demanded. 'If it was so expensive and unusual, why haven't we asked the local angling society who has one? I'll do it tomorrow. And we should follow up the blue-film ticket, but I'm not volunteering for that.'

The atmosphere became uneasy again. Mitchell asked quietly, his words carefully separated, 'What blue-film ticket?'

Zoe sighed. She had meant to insist that the police were told about the bag that Cameron had removed from Crowther's locker but she had not meant to drop the information carelessly into the conversation so as to cause Benny maximum annoyance.

Cameron was defiant as he described his actions. 'If your guys hadn't been so rude, I'd have handed it over—maybe. But I'd seen him push that stuff hurriedly away. I only wanted his sordid little secrets to remain secret.'

Benny's voice was still dangerously quiet. 'What if the bag had contained material that Crowther was using for blackmail purposes? How do I know, in fact, that it didn't, that you haven't taken something out of it and just left us the rest of the garbage to look through? How do I know you haven't planted the film ticket?'

Frank appeared in the kitchen doorway. 'Just a minute. Isn't the ticket in Graham's name?'

Benny was contemptuous. 'Did whoever gave a name when he paid for it have to show a birth certificate?'

Zoe had had enough. 'Go and have your little boys' argument somewhere else.' She flung open the door and Mitchell and Cameron walked meekly through it.

Frank made to follow. 'Not you, idiot! I thought you wanted your lunch. By the way, you can't come here for tea. I'll be having it with Jeffie Lister's aunt. She invited me when she rang up.'

'How will you get in.'

'Up a ramp and a widened doorway. She's an amputee in a wheelchair, according to Margaret. What are you looking so puzzled about?'

Frank helped himself to one of the mugs of coffee that were no longer required. 'I was wondering why having kept your investigation a secret till now, you suddenly decided to be up-front about it.'

'Because, at the funeral, Linda told everyone who would listen that she and Graham were having problems and that I had been counselling her. That left the way open for me.'

'And how was the funeral?'

'You might say he had a good send-off. I've seen less alcohol served at a wedding.' By the time lunch was cooked and eaten, Frank was privy to the information Zoe had received from the funeral guests on Monday and from Peter that morning. He surprised her by insisting that Mitchell should hear the whole story at once. Zoe disagreed.

'I'm not sure he's right. I'm not even sure he isn't making it all up, though I don't think so.'

'That's Benny's problem.' Frank was about to demonstrate the strength of his conviction by dialling the number himself but Zoe's glance gave him second thoughts.

She propelled her chair towards the instrument but stopped in front of it and turned back to him. 'There's something I've never told you—or anyone—because I wasn't sure. On the night of my accident, we saw two men running away from the flat before we rounded the others up. I think one of them was Leon Glasby.'

Mary Lister was watching from the window as Zoe's car drew up outside her house. She waved and disappeared but the door slid open before she could possibly have wheeled herself into the hall.

As she manoeuvred herself into her chair and secured her car, Zoe wondered about the possible advantages of this amenity in her own house. The topic nicely broke the ice as Mrs Lister welcomed her. 'Depends whether you have as many disabled visitors as I do,' she was told, briskly. 'Do come through. This is a biggish hall, but opening the door, then moving back to allow another chair to get in, and then getting round that to close it again was such a cumbersome business that I decided the electric door wasn't really an extravagance.'

The tea, however, set out on a table in the living-room, certainly was. Zoe regarded the luscious iced fruit-cake, buttered scones and crumpets, and then the lean portions of her hostess, visible above the rug across her lap. Did she not have the same physically inactive life as herself and therefore the same need to eat sparingly to avoid becoming gross?

Mrs Lister followed her eyes and laughed. 'Yes, I do need to watch my diet but I don't impose it on my visitors. I didn't realize we shared the problem, otherwise...'

Zoe was astonished. 'You mean Margaret didn't give you my life history and say how nice it would be for both of us to have a little talk about all our problems?'

'She is a bit patronizing, I agree, but she means well. My sharp tongue has taught her to bite hers. Let's eat before the crumpets are cold. We'll both have to make an exception or my afternoon will have been wasted.'

They ate and talked comfortably. From her telephone conversation with Mrs Lister, Zoe had been expecting her to be somewhat mentally decayed as well as physically handicapped. She was proving to be far otherwise. Maybe she just hated the telephone. In answer to quite direct questions, Zoe was soon describing, with a readiness that astonished her, the trauma of first finding herself paralysed.

In the past two years she had adamantly refused to join any club, group or activity 'for the disabled'. She did not belong to a race apart. She would participate on equal terms or not at all. Here though was an intelligent individual who could understand exactly what she wanted to say, who shared her new values.

'In spinal shock, straight after the accident, I was almost totally paralysed. I needed artificial respiration. It was very frightening not to be able to feel my own body. Only my face and head had any sensation at first. I knew I was attached to the respirator but I couldn't feel my chest move and I kept convincing myself that I wasn't breathing and was about to die.

'Then when the mental confusion subsided, questions started up in my head. What's happened? Why can't I move? What about my bladder and bowels?' She grinned at her hostess. 'I've talked about them more in the last two years than in all the rest of my life. The physical exposure was very embarrassing at first.'

She bit absently into another scone. 'Then I got to the stage when, having lost such a lot and faced it, what I regained made me feel very positive. After not being able to blow my nose or powder it, getting back to washing and feeding myself made me feel quite capable and independent.

'Eventually, when progress seemed to have stopped, I asked if I was going to recover any more. I knew the answer really but it was still pretty shattering to be condemned to a wheelchair.'

'What did you do?'

Zoe sighed. 'For a while I gave my friends and relations hell. I told my mother not to interfere and I told Frank to go.'

'Did he?'

Zoe shook her head. 'Let's wash up,' she suggested. Talking was easier when your hands were busy. Between them they cleared the dishes efficiently without further conversation. As she handed Zoe a drying cloth, Mrs Lister remarked, 'When you get home, you have a tendency to try to resume life as it was before. It takes time to adjust to a new code of living. You and your relatives have to live through a period of grief because the old person has died. The new one, in some ways, is somebody else...I hope I haven't upset you.'

For a moment, Zoe was unable to speak, even to offer the necessary reassurance. Her hostess waited patiently, watching her dry a cup with unnecessary thoroughness. When she was ready she put it down on the work-surface. 'You've just put in a nutshell the reason I can't marry Frank...'

Suddenly, Zoe changed the subject, unsure whether she had just remembered her manners or whether she was unwilling to expose herself any more. 'Tell me what happened to you.'

Mrs Lister was matter-of-fact. 'A road accident. I had my right leg amputated.'

'And did it spoil your relationship with your husband?'

'Drastically. He was killed.' She cut short Zoe's embarrassed apology. 'In a way, I'm glad. You and I were strong enough to build new lives. Dick would have lost everything he lived for if he'd just been injured. He'd always been very active, a sportsman. As he got older, he took especial pride in beating younger men. He wasn't musical, he rarely read anything. He would have found even a hale and hearty old age difficult to fill.

'I miss him greatly but, if I'm honest, I have to admit that I'd have found his depressing company very hard to bear—when he became elderly and failing, or, worse, disabled.'

Such honesty gave Zoe the courage to admit, 'Things between us are at an all-time low at the moment.'

'Any particular reason?'

Zoe hung the cloth to dry. 'Two particular reasons. He's fed up with being turned down—eight times now—and...'

'You don't have to go on,' Mrs Lister assured her after some moments of silence. But Zoe needed an impartial ear and, having come so far, was determined to go all the way. Her hostess listened without comment until Zoe was silent once more. Then she startled her by asking, 'Are you secretly attracted to this coach?'

Zoe made herself give the question serious consideration. Was that why she had let Frank's resentment drift on unchallenged? She was very much afraid so. Rob was extraordinarily good-looking but he had none of Frank's sensitivity. He purported to be Graham Crowther's friend but his remarks about him were often very cutting and he had no sympathies with Linda that were not crowded out by his dislike of her. But yes, she was attracted to him. She hung her head.

Mrs Lister smiled. 'And he's smitten too?'

'I think he might be, a little.'

'And he only knows you in your present condition, so you know he finds you attractive as you are now.' Zoe sat very still. 'If he does, why not Frank?' She received no answer. 'What does *he* look like? Have you got a photograph?'

Zoe groped in the pouch which hung from the arm of the wheelchair and handed over a snapshot. The older woman studied it for almost a minute. 'Was it you behind the lens? I bet he doesn't give that lecherous grin to the victims of distemper and cat flu. You've known him a long time, haven't you? I think it was his misfortune to have met you before the accident happened. He's part of the old life that you're trying of necessity to cast off. You've decided that the Brave New Start can't include him. Why not? You haven't rejected your parents.'

'No, but I have a new relationship with them.'

'Fine. Have a new one with Frank.'

'That's all right from my point of view, but Frank liked things as they were before.'

Mrs Lister tutted impatiently. 'So did you. You've had the wisdom, courage and determination to adjust. Why are you not willing to credit *him* with those qualities? Are you so fond of facing difficulties head-on, so set on facing the worst and dealing with it, that Frank has to be made an example of?

'Sweet stuff makes you thirsty when you're not used to it,' Mrs Lister went on with hardly a pause. 'I'll brew up again.'

It seemed to Zoe that the kettle took a tactfully long time to reboil. After such revelations, what subjects could be taboo between them? Zoe found herself listening to some of Mary Lister's troubles, including the sorry story of the seduction of Mrs Lister's great-niece when she was still a schoolgirl, and the backstreet abortion that the father had procured for her. Neither set of parents had known anything about it until the results had threatened Jennifer's life.

Zoe was shocked. She remembered Jeffie's long absence from school, chiefly because she had been the one to deputize for her in the school production of *The Gondoliers*. She had been just fourteen and had believed Jeffie's parents' explanation for her serious illness, though she could no longer remember what it had been. At the time, she had been taken up only with the twin worries of whether she would acquit herself musically without disgrace and whether she would be considered an upstart for replacing an august member of the lower sixth when she was only a fourth-former. 'You must be thankful that she made such a good recovery.'

Zoe saw from the aunt's face that the recovery had not been so complete as she had supposed. 'She's healthy enough now, but there won't be any more babies. That's left her with as many inhibitions about getting married as you have. And, whilst Jennifer fled Cloughton and the disgrace—for it was still a disgrace even so few years ago—the young man struts shamelessly around and leers at us from the pages of the *Clarion*, as many nights as not, proclaiming his good deeds.'

'Leon Glasby!'

'The same. Though his father is as

much to blame as the boy. He's a very successful businessman, but sadly lacking in the parenting department. You look surprised. Did the "Leon is a son to be proud of" charade take you in? I suppose you weren't to know. Leon had a very silver tongue, won public-speaking competitions...'

'And travel scholarships with essays on banking and business that dear Daddy had written for him! His exam results proved what a fraud he was. I remember him getting a less welcome mention in the *Clarion* just after he left school, as being "innocently pulled to the fringe of" activities that sent his associates to prison. I wonder how much that little perversion of the truth cost his father? I just looked surprised because...well, I don't want to offend you but Leon is only a couple of months older than me.'

'Yes, and Jennifer's three years older, but the boy was tall and handsome and as smooth as only a great deal too much money could make him. Jennifer soon saw sense but not quickly enough. If the brute hadn't scared her into secrecy, she could have had a perfectly legal and safe operation organized by her parents.'

'Was she afraid of them?'

'No, she was afraid of her classmates knowing that she'd had a relationship with a cocky fourth-former. She's confident and successful and attractive now, but she was a queer little object at seventeen and had hardly even spoken to a boy. If only her parents had lived to see her success.'

'Another accident?'

'No, they were turned forty when Jennifer was born. Jenny's isn't a long-lived family.'

They passed to pleasanter topics and drained the teapot for a second time before Zoe insisted she had to leave. The necklace was duly handed over and temporarily secured in the wheelchair pouch, after Zoe had admired it and heard the history of its passage through the generations of the Lister family. Profuse thanks were offered and plans made to meet again as the sliding door was finally activated. Mrs Lister kissed Zoe's cheek in grandmotherly fashion. 'Go home, and when your young man comes calling imagine you met him just yesterday. Concentrate on your feelings now and take it from there.'

Zoe was obedient to the spirit rather than the letter of the instructions. When Frank arrived, later that evening, he bounded into the kitchen and found that the cooker was cold.

'We're eating out,' Zoe announced.

'Are we celebrating something?'

Zoe smiled. 'I'm not sure yet. It depends

what you have to say to my proposal. Will you marry me? I'm afraid I'm not so patient as you, so, if you turn me down, I don't think I can screw myself up to asking you again.'

Much later, they agreed that the meal had qualified as a celebration, even though neither of them had eaten more than half of it.

Chapter Ten

Detective Constable Mitchell was at a familiar crossroads in his current case. He knew who had committed the crime, how, when, where. All he needed now were a few bits of confirmatory evidence, and he had spent his afternoon in an unmarked car, watching for two of his suspects to make a rendezvous. Neither had turned up.

DC Mitchell had theories about why not, and about how the warning had been given, ideas about his next move and visions of future glory, but, this sharp and damp late afternoon, all he felt was a restless dissatisfaction with his day's achievements. He was in just the mood, he recognized, to go off, as was his wont, and against protocol, on some exploit that would earn him a reprimand, but also earmark him as a rising, if slightly unconventional, star.

He'd drop in at the Blue Rose and see what they could tell him. After all, it was almost on his way home—if he went the long way round through Leeds. He parked nonchalantly in the visitors' car-park of the local police station and soon found the mean little street, leading between tall buildings away from the main shopping thoroughfare.

The door he sought was half-way down, discreetly indicated by a turquoise neon sign, too small to be made out by the uninitiated. A flight of stone steps led down to a basement hallway. Two doors led from it on one side and an opening was set into the wall on the other where a uniformed man scrutinized him from behind a counter. Mitchell paid the required entry fee and tried to analyse the general impression of scruffiness although nothing was actually dirty.

The uniformed man received his money ungratefully, peered at it suspiciously and issued a small purple ticket. Mitchell thought he was more likely to recognize the banknote again than his own face. The films were being shown in the room accessible from the farther door. Mitchell found a seat, watched for a few minutes and saw nothing that excited him. He spent a further few minutes in pitying the specimens of humanity around him who had to substitute this for a satisfying relationship with a real woman.

After a while the titillating images faded temporarily. The lights above the transparent false ceiling increased in strength enough to take the room from almost dark to dim, and Mitchell suddenly recognized the avid viewer, pony-tailed and leather-jacketed, who was sitting next to him.

When Linda Crowther next tapped on Zoe's rather battered office door, the corridor echoed with muffled music escaping from within. So far as Zoe knew, Jeffie Lister had not recorded any of the songs she would sing at this week's concert. On being consulted, Glyn Morgan had offered his daughter the loan of a tape featuring two of them, rendered by Isobel Baillie.

Linda's nose wrinkled as she went into the office. 'I don't think we have musical tastes in common,' she announced.

Zoe turned the sound lower. 'Perhaps it would have been more in Graham's line.'

Linda sniffed. 'You're joking. Actually, we never listened to any kind of music much, not at home, though Graham sometimes went to a concert with Rob, to give the impression of being cultured. We did learn to endure Peter's pop music though, and now I find that nursery rhymes on tape keep Helena quiet for a few minutes at a time, for which I'm profoundly thankful.'

Zoe switched off the tape. 'I think we should talk about Helena today,' she suggested as she watched Linda arrange herself in the uncomfortable clients' armchair. She noted that the silver grey had been abandoned in favour of an elegant thin wool suit in a blackberry shade with a cream silk shirt. Zoe watched her crossing slim ankles to show off slender-heeled cream court shoes. Not quite right, Zoe decided, for either the season or the rest of the outfit.

'Why?' Aggressively.

'Because I think you may be trying to cut out perfectly natural feelings about her that you think are wrong, even wicked.' The aggression became resignation as Zoe continued, 'Did you know during the pregnancy that you were carrying a Down's child?'

Linda shrugged and laughed mirthlessly. 'Some idiot told me it's not a disease but part of our rich and varied biological inheritance!'

Some comment was obviously expected. 'I suppose it would be totally unrealistic to imagine that an affected child will cause no problems. You haven't answered me.'

Linda scowled at her twisting fingers. 'I went for the test. They made two attempts to draw off some fluid. I would have had to go back two weeks later but I decided against it. The needle in my stomach was too threatening. It didn't hurt but it invaded my privacy.' She seemed to feel that this was an adequate explanation and glared at Zoe defiantly.

Zoe stared at the blank grey side of her filing cabinet and counted to ten. 'So, your fears became reality. How did it all work out?'

'There was no problem about accepting her newly born. She was quite appealing then.' Zoe noted the converse that was implied. 'She didn't look odd, except that she didn't look as much like either of us as Peter had done.

'When the doctor broke the news to us, I could see that Graham was knocked sideways. Looking back, I think I was concentrating on not embarrassing anyone with any display of emotion, and hating and despising Graham for giving way. I was terrified that someone would put their arms round me, comfort me.'

'Why?'

'That would have repulsed and frightened me. I can't cope with sympathy. I like coming here. You're abrasive.'

'Am I? I don't mean to be.'

'Well, for God's sake don't change. I need you like that.' After a moment, she reverted to her story. 'There was all this technical talk about the way they recognize the syndrome. I could cope with that and I listened carefully. They told me about the

171

characteristics Helena had, about the blood work that they were doing, the possibility of a stomach blockage and heart problems. Then a doctor said, "If you're going to have a handicapped child, it's the best handicap to have"!'

The laughter was harsh and suddenly Linda was weeping. Was this the breakthrough? Zoe longed to approach her, take her hand, hug her, but didn't dare. As she debated with herself, Linda scrubbed her face angrily and continued speaking, her voice firm again.

'I asked a lot of questions. What kind of heart problems? How should we take care of her? I thought I was being strong, but telling myself it didn't matter was just as weak as Graham's crying, I suppose.'

Zoe decided she could not endure another diatribe against Graham. 'How did Peter react?'

She looked surprised at the change of tack. 'He was sixteen and very rebellious towards a new sibling until she was born. Then, suddenly, because she wasn't normal, or because she was a girl, he took an enormous interest. I didn't feel we had to worry about the effect on Peter. He'd had his childhood, and before Helena was much more than a toddler he'd be away. It had been obvious for some time that he would go to university.' Her voice was toneless and betrayed nothing of her attitude to her son.

'Do you think Graham was a good parent to Peter?'

Linda wrinkled her nose. 'There weren't any comparable problems so I didn't notice at the time. He took his usual line of least resistance to his adolescent behaviour. Peter came home once saying he'd been offered drugs by a schoolfriend. Graham thought that, once he'd told him to keep well away from that kind of thing, the danger had been dealt with. I made enquiries and found out who was supplying the stuff to the boy's father. I made Graham go and confront him...'

'Just a minute. Are we talking about Councillor Glasby?'

Linda's fingers twisted a button. 'Don't say I said so. Anyway, he denied it. Even tried to blame the young chap from the canoe club. That upset Graham. He was quite fond of Rob, went off to tell him about the slander and urge him to take some action.'

Laura Gibson tapped on Zoe's door as usual to discuss her client's progress. 'I'm not checking up on you. This woman's got me interested in her by proxy, just from what you've said about her.'

Zoe was reluctant to share her impressions, which had not yet settled into an opinion about what she had been listening to. 'I'm sure having the little Down's girl is responsible for a lot of her problems. I wish I had some way of knowing what the marriage was like before she was thought of. Looking back now, Linda paints it all black but I'm not sure. She talks a bit about her feelings for her son but she only mentions her daughter as a series of problems.

'Helena seemed to be the last subject she wanted to talk about first, then, when she began, a great dam burst. Though somehow all the admissions seemed reluctant, against her better judgement.'

'You think she was feeling guilty for not loving the child enough?'

Zoe shook her head. 'I just don't know yet. She's upset by Helena's physical unattractiveness. She doesn't like taking her out.'

'She isn't a flattering accessory?'

'That's the impression I got, but I suppose the child's difficult to control and it's awkward in public places.' Zoe fell silent, unable to explain even to herself the mixture of pity and censure she felt.

'Does she miss her husband's support?'

Zoe considered. 'I think she does, but she doesn't realize it. She doesn't consider he was supportive. He showed his feelings when the child was born. Linda decided that he was weak and she would have to be doubly strong. She set superhuman standards for the child, no messy eating and so on. She knows Helena isn't capable of the level of behaviour she expects and so she had no sympathy with Graham's wish to stimulate the child, give her the best quality of life possible. According to Linda, he made all the mistakes and all tedious, unpleasant tasks were left to her.

'Actually, she doesn't seem to have been willing to accept much help. She seems to think the offers are grudging. If she does need to depend on someone else, she has to justify it. "Just this once", or "Of course she was just a baby at the time, hardly any trouble." Then, when people get tired of being snubbed and turned down, she sulks because she has little respite. I think she almost enjoys her resentment now.'

'Or maybe she thinks temporary help is just an insult, that the burden should be removed for good.'

Zoe looked up, startled. 'I think you may have hit the nail on the head!'

It was with relief that she watched Laura depart. She felt restless, in need of some distracting occupation. Almost immediately, the phone shrilled on her desk.

Her hand reached out wearily towards it but her spirits lifted as she listened to Mitchell's voice. She made encouraging replies. 'Have you now? What were they all watching? Did it make your hair curl?

'Leon? Well, I can't say I'm surprised. Thanks for letting me know. No, there's nothing else "that great canoeing oaf" has told me that I haven't told you. If that's how you address him, I'm not surprised he withholds evidence.' She chatted for a further few minutes, then put the receiver down, her usual sanguine attitude to life restored. She would go to see Leon—for old times' sake.

It was already five-thirty. She had to be properly equipped and reporting in for her second canoeing lesson by half past seven. The journey to Leon's house would take an incalculable time in the rush-hour traffic. Besides, her visit ought to be carefully planned so as to make the best use of such knowledge as she already had, in order to obtain more.

All the time she argued with herself, she knew underneath that she would go. As the decision became a conscious one, she realized that she had stowed away the detritus of the afternoon's interviews, locked her filing cabinet and was ready to depart.

Her subconscious mind had her journey ready-planned. She avoided the worst of the traffic by skirting the town centre and going through the suburb village of Heathfield to Crossley Bridge. She knew she had always been good at playing a situation by ear, and therefore rehearsed the facts at her disposal rather than planning her attack.

It had been Leon, according to the doorman Benny had spoken to, who had introduced Graham Crowther to the Blue Rose. It had been Leon who, according to Mary Lister, had seduced Jeffie, arranged the abortion that had denied her the experience of motherhood and driven her away from Cloughton. It had been someone with the initials L.G who had supplied the Festival Hall concert ticket that was to have taken Graham to London to—what? Hear Jeffie sing? It seemed unlikely in view of Linda's reaction to her taped music, and as far as Zoe knew Graham and Jeffie had never met.

Suddenly, as she had known it would, the perfect excuse for her call on Leon occurred to Zoe. It would irritate him, perhaps make him unwise in his later conversation. At the next safe spot she parked, fished out a notebook and began to scribble. Satisfied after a few moments, she tore out the page, folded it and stowed it in her jacket pocket.

Leon heard Zoe's car as it drew up in the drive. She felt irritated as he came to the front door and watched her manoeuvre her chair. She concentrated on the levers, anxious that the irritation should not show as a clumsiness that would allow him to pity her.

He greeted her with apparent pleasure. 'Zoe! What a surprise. Knowing you, I don't suppose you've come to express appreciation of the leisure-centre ramp.'

Zoe regarded him sardonically. 'You don't know me but you're right.' She scowled at the two steps leading up to his front door. 'I was looking forward to a chat. What a pity you can't personally accommodate wheelchair-bound guests!'

He was smug. 'On the contrary.' With a flourish, he activated the up-and-over door of his garage. He preceded her through it and unlocked a wide door that gave access to his entrance hall. 'The dining-room has a french window with its sliding mechanism sunk into the floor, so that you could also enjoy the delights of the patio in spite of the steps down to the garden. However, as it's a chilly evening, shall we use the sitting-room instead?'

This proved to be a widening-out of the hall. Leon pushed aside a buttoned, soft-leather armchair, so that the wheelchair could park next to his own. Zoe did not

178

begrudge him his mocking amusement. What she had observed during her few seconds' passage through the garage had made her visit worthwhile even if she left now.

She accepted his invitation to share his Yorkshire high tea. 'I prefer it to a later dinner,' he explained, 'partly because it annoys my father who thinks it's plebeian, and partly because it leaves the evening free for all my good works.'

'And your various hobbies and pastimes.'

'And those,' he agreed equably.

Zoe surveyed him critically. Since she had last seen him, the pony-tail had become thinner and sadder. He remained lean, though his figure was flattered by the cut of jeans that she knew had cost him—or his father—a sum in excess of her week's housekeeping. The waistcoat which restrained just a hint of middle-age spread brought to Zoe's mind a phrase from a favourite childhood story. Like the Parsee man's hat, it reflected the rays of the sun in more than oriental splendour.

As they made polite tea-time conversation, Zoe was highly entertained by Leon's increasing uneasiness. She could see he was irritated by her ingratitude towards him and he seemed anxious about the apparent pointlessness of her visit. She accepted a slice of apple pie, refused

179

cream, then put him temporarily out of his misery by producing the scrap of paper from her jacket pocket.

'I came to bring you this. It's my personal list of places I want to visit in Cloughton but where I'm denied access because of steps. I thought it would be a good follow-up to the piece in the *Clarion* last week if you got all the Cloughton paraplegics to compile their own similar lists, worked out where the need was greatest and ran a campaign to pressurize the people concerned into doing something about it.'

He was happy again. 'Brilliant! Will you be photographed with me?'

'No chance, but I'm sure you'll soon find someone who will, and the *Clarion* will be delighted to feature you yet again. I'm much too busy this week. I went to have tea on Tuesday with Mary Lister, Jeffie's aunt. Do you remember Jeffie?'

He regarded her suspiciously though his tone remained light. 'Certainly do. We had a bit of a fling at one time, though the old girl didn't approve of me.'

'Well, you aren't exactly her type. Mrs Lister is very fond of Jeffie. Frank and I are going to hear her sing in London tomorrow night so I'll be too busy to pose for newspaper photographs anyway—unless they want to do a feature on Cloughton's

180

famous children. You know, then and now. Perhaps you could feature in that too.'

'What are you up to, Zoe?'

She smiled sweetly. 'I'm up to collecting information. Benny Mitchell tells me you introduced Graham Crowther to the Blue Rose. Why?'

'Why not? The poor devil was getting sod-all at home.'

'Enjoy himself there, did he?'

'Not sure he did, much. He'd have been quite happy with the missionary position twice a week. He told me he sometimes wondered if the little girl was his punishment for raping his wife. I thought the poor-sex-starved-husband pose was just one of his tales but I believed him after a bit.'

Zoe waved away a second helping of pie. 'You must have known him well to have discussed such intimate aspects of his marriage.'

Leon shook his head. 'No one ever took any notice of him in a crowd so he specialized in shocking revelations on a one-to-one basis. When he ran out of factual ones he made them up.'

'So I gather. Apparently you featured in some of them. How did you meet him?'

His grin was obviously an effort. 'Being a good Samaritan, as usual. Fixed the child a place at the Opportunities Playgroup.'

181

'Fixed it? Wouldn't she qualify anyway?'

He shrugged. 'No harm in letting the poor lad think he had a friend who wanted to do him a kindness.'

'Big of you. Why did you do him the kindness of getting him a ticket for Jeffie's concert tomorrow? He wouldn't have been grateful. He apparently had about as much appreciation of the fine arts as you have.'

The slight produced no discernible reaction but the further mention of Jeffie rattled him. 'If he hadn't topped himself, you could have asked him, even gone with him.'

'Did he ever talk about topping himself?'

'No, but isn't that what you and your portly PC friend are sniffing around for? Anyway, I don't know anything about any concert ticket.'

Zoe had known him for a long time and thought she knew when to believe him.

When his guest made departing noises, Leon made no attempt to detain her. 'I'm most grateful for the meal, Leon,' she had told him airily. 'Besides being delicious, it means I shan't be late for my canoeing lesson now that I don't have to prepare anything.'

He had closed the door without watching her into her car. She credited him with no manners, so she would get no benefit from his assistance. Canoeing, though. He had to hand it to her.

Thoughtfully, he gathered up the dirty dishes. How much did she know and about what? It would be more than he liked if she knew the Crowthers, but surely not much that she could prove. If she'd seen him, as he'd feared at the time, escaping from the Cooper Street flat at the time of the drugs bust, she'd never have left it so long before taking action. It was very likely just the business with Jeffie. Now he must dream up a damage-limitation scheme. He wasn't sure what Zoe was up to. Was it some sort of punishment for his patronizing or teasing her? But he'd been doing that since they were both eleven, and, though she was a conceited bitch, always full of herself, she had never been spiteful.

What would carrying out her implied threat gain for her? Surely it had to be something worth more than his dishing the dirt on that pathetic oaf Crowther. Was she working for fat Mitchell, something a bit dodgy that His Constableship might get the push for?

He had to admit to himself that he enjoyed his reputation for having been a bit of a lad, but, if Zoe had had all the details of the Lister affair from the point of view of the indignant aunt and was determined to get them published...

183

Thank the Lord he's always kept on the right side of the *Clarion* lot. The thing would be to get in first. Perhaps he could get old Hendy to do his profile earlier than planned. Maybe next week.

Abandoning the washing-up, he reached for the telephone.

Chapter Eleven

Emerging from the changing room, Zoe rolled down to the riverbank and waited for someone to be free to help get her launched. She knew, because Frank had told her, that the bustling and rustling in the undergrowth behind her was probably a fox, intent on his courting.

Her surmise was immediately vindicated and she giggled as the shriek of the vixen made the youngsters good-naturedly hurrying to help her, almost jump out of their skins. There followed the high-pitched barking of the dog, normally cautious but distracted now by lust. They were not the serious screams of pain that she and Frank had sometimes heard on winter-evening strolls, that told of bitten ears and legs as fights broke out between rivals.

She called out merely, 'It's all right, only foxes.' Frank had mentioned the youngsters' ironic thanks for the biology lecture when he had forgotten himself and tried to share his fascination with the riverside wildlife.

Frank was not canoeing tonight, she explained when Cameron enquired for him. 'He's at the huge birthday party his sister always stages. I use the verb advisedly!'

'Shouldn't you be there too?'

'Yes. I got him to make my excuses. I'm keen to follow up on last weeks' progress and I've no patience with Anne-Marie's actressy friends.'

'Is that what she does?'

'Yes, she's in local rep. It's regular work and good training but she's good and deserves a bigger break.'

'But you don't like her?'

'I've nothing in common with her.'

He nodded. 'What do you say to our nipping off on our own tonight, giving the crowd the slip? We can't have them eavesdropping while you give me the details of your fascinating day.'

Zoe sighed. 'I'm not discussing any of it tonight. There's been nothing new since I rang you. I want a break from vicious Linda and feckless Graham and the unfortunate Peter and Helena.'

'Have you rung Mr Plod?'

'I don't know a Mr Plod.' She raised her voice and made its tone warmer. 'I could use a bit of help wriggling into this death-trap.'

The youngsters came forward and, following Cameron's instructions, soon had Zoe safely installed in her kayak.

She was glad to concentrate on the physical challenge and had no trouble in banishing the Crowthers and all their affairs from her mind. This week she was determined to learn how to travel forward, and her first attempt at going straight proved very frustrating. The boat veered off course, apparently without reason, and infuriatingly refused to return.

Zoe applied persistence, brute force and logic. None of them worked. Eventually, she realized that the path followed by even the comparative experts was not a straight line but a zigzag course as they paddled first left, then right. She watched more carefully and worked out that the back of the boat swung more than the front, so that each swing had to match exactly the preceding one. It was as much a creative art as an exercise in engineering.

Cameron pointed out a tree stump embedded in the far bank. 'Line up the bow exactly with that and watch out for when you move off course from it. Stop worrying about proper paddling. Just use short pushes to each side, well out from the kayak. For novices it's very difficult to recognize when a boat is starting to turn until it's too late and a big uncontrollable spin has already started. The knack is to learn to detect the boat's movement earlier and react faster...'

Canoeing finesse was slow in coming, but Zoe had already become an expert at translating verbose kayakese into brief clear instructions of her own that she could follow. She let the details of the technique for stopping float over her head, extracting the essentials that made up her own version. 'Make a couple of reverse strokes, short and fast.' It worked.

She tried to follow Cameron's instructions to use all the muscles in her upper body to paddle more effectively. 'The more muscles you use, the less each one has to do, and it encourages a more flexible style. It's a fundamental aspect, not just a refinement.' This observation depressed Zoe a little. If her strength and stability in the boat were dependent on leg movement, she would never be a very good canoeist. Having proved she could make a stab at it did she want to put in all the effort it would take to become mediocre?

Sensing her discouragement, Cameron reassured her. 'You're very versatile. It always annoys me to see people stubbornly sticking to something that clearly isn't working and making ineffective dabs with the paddle instead of letting it flow. You can't do some things the orthodox way but you're learning to improvise very effectively.'

Zoe was comforted. However, she was

growing wary of Cameron's compliments. Once they were all comfortably established in the pub, safely surrounded by a dozen or so paddlers, she deliberately displayed her reacquired ring for everyone's admiration.

Frank appeared on Friday morning at the early hour they had appointed. Zoe suspected that he was at least a little hung-over, but he described the antics of his sister's party guests for her entertainment as they began their journey.

'She didn't mind my not being there?'

Frank confirmed Zoe's suspicion that her absence had in no way diminished Anne-Marie's enjoyment of the celebration. 'You weren't necessary for the effect she wanted to create. How did you disport yourself?' Zoe described Mitchell's discovery of Leon Glasby's predilection for pornographic films and her own visit to his house. 'Any joy?'

'There was a Hardy fishing-rod, hanging on the wall of his garage.' Frank mimed a whistle as he negotiated the slip road on to the M1. 'He offered me a slice of delicious spiced apple pie. I asked him for the recipe so I could compare his writing with that on the note sent with the concert ticket. It didn't look a lot like it.'

'Pity. I hoped it was so you could make the pie for me.'

'I'll have a go.' She giggled. 'I can't quite see Leon peering into the oven to check if his pastry's browning.'

'Perhaps he only claimed to have made it.'

'No, he had the recipe in his head. Didn't have to reach for the book. And he had a smug look because he'd managed to surprise me.' She glared through the windscreen whilst Frank drove another mile.

'Penny for them.'

'I was wondering what possible connection there could be between Jeffie and Leon and Graham Crowther, and why, whatever it is, it should lead to Graham's death.'

'You're abandoning Linda as a suspect, then?'

'I haven't abandoned anyone but I'm not discussing Linda any more except when any information about her has come from the person I'm talking to. What I get at Relate is off limits. It's my turn to drive. Stop at the next service station.'

Frank did so gladly, and dosed his hangover with coffee and aspirin. When Zoe took the wheel he closed his eyes and dozed. He had had barely four hours' sleep and he knew that she rarely chatted when driving.

Zoe slipped confidently into a space

between a Yorkshire Rider coach and a decrepit and elderly Ford on the inside lane of the motorway, and drove as smoothly as possible until she was sure that Frank was fast asleep. She wanted an hour or so alone with her own thoughts before facing her evening's entertainment.

She was becoming more and more willing to believe that Linda Crowther might have killed her husband, not by a deliberate decision but in a frenzy of frustration. And she was less and less willing to deliver her up for judgement or punishment. Perhaps it would throw new light on the matter if she stopped trying to see things from Linda's point of view and tried instead to clarify her picture of Graham.

She had to remember that everything she had been told about him was coloured by the opinions of her informants, especially his wife. She remained certain that Linda had had some purpose in seeking counselling and sharing confidences about her husband, other than wanting to improve their relationship and to sort out her own feelings. All the same, Zoe felt that Linda's despair about her lack of spontaneity and the history of the meeting and subsequent marriage had, on the whole, been honestly described.

Graham had met Linda as a student

teacher and asked her to go walking in the country with him. He had been physically rebuffed and yet he had proposed marriage to her—and, when refused, he had persevered until she had accepted him. Why? Had he recognized in Linda a fellow-victim, crippled by life's experiences? Had he been deceived by her apparent docility, her extreme modesty, into thinking that here was a woman who would not threaten him? How soon, she wondered, had he been undeceived, and realized how she despised him?

And how much had her contempt upset and undermined him? He had used fairy-stories as a drug, for relief and a little excitement, till they had become addictive and he had lived in a fantasy world. That was not necessarily Linda's fault. According to the whisky-swilling funeral guest, Graham had been a 'lying little toad' since he was a small child.

Had he lied to Linda? She had complained only of the painful embarrassment of his and her friends knowing that what he told them was not true. It struck Zoe that she had not thought about *their* friends'. They seemed not to have had friends in common as a couple. Linda, in fact, had so far not mentioned a specific friend. Still, no one would have killed him because he told lies. In fact, his stories seemed to have

192

afforded some of his acquaintances a good deal of amusement.

Could his death really have been a simple accident? Whilst Frank had been doing his stint of driving, Zoe had idly pulled out from the pouch in the car-door lining his October copy of *Canoeist*. By coincidence, there on the cover was a picture of an expert performing a pirouette. The details which she had vaguely apprehended when Rob Cameron described them suddenly became quite clear. The frail, slender craft stood on its tip. Inside, its occupant's feet pointed to the sky and his gaze was directed towards them. His back stuck out at right angles to the boat, parallel to the surface of the water that surged and boiled below him. Doubtless his paddle was being expertly employed to help achieve the manoeuvre safely but it seemed to Zoe that he was using it to attract the attention of the Almighty in a desperate appeal for rescue.

There seemed no way that the man she had been studying so carefully through the eyes of others would be capable of risking his life in this manner. The only suggestion that he might have done so was in the note which Linda claimed he had left for her, and which no one else had seen.

What kind of father had Graham been? According to Linda and Cameron, he had been upset and disappointed when Helena's condition became apparent, but he had accepted it and learned to love her. And his son? Perhaps Peter had been more of a threat, enough to cause Graham to try to establish himself as a rival in Rachel's affections. The lies must have been very humiliating to Peter. Could he have been murderously angry about them?

She didn't know what to make of Peter. The purpose of his visit to her seemed very nebulous. She hadn't sensed any real concern for his mother. Was he afraid for her mental health, maybe anxious that if she were imprisoned or hospitalized he would have to take responsibility for his sister? She dismissed this idea. He wouldn't expect that burden at barely twenty.

She signalled and moved into the fast lane to overtake a cluster of slower vehicles. Frank grunted and slid further towards her but he didn't wake. Soon he would, so in the meantime she had better face her main problem squarely. How did Rob Cameron fit into all this? She wanted to believe that he didn't fit at all and she wanted to know why it mattered to her. Her renewed engagement represented a firm commitment to her own future with Frank and she'd expected that, with this decision made, her attraction to Rob would disappear. If anything, it had become stronger. Would marriage, she wondered, be like this? Perhaps, even safe in a happy and fulfilled relationship, she would always be vulnerable to her flirtatious nature whenever she met a personable male.

She braked sharply as a van cut in discourteously in front of her. The car jolted them both and, with an undignified snort, Frank roused, rubbed his eyes and decreed it was lunch-time.

Zoe nodded. 'It's twenty miles to the next service station. Tell me what you think of Rob Cameron.' Frank blinked at her sleepily. 'Is he capable of killing Graham Crowther?'

Frank was thunderstruck. 'Rob? Of course not. Why should he? They were friends...'

'Did it strike you as a very likely friendship?'

'If this is how you talk when you're driving, thank goodness you're usually silent.'

'You're avoiding the question.'

Zoe had driven another mile before Frank admitted reluctantly, 'I suppose it wasn't, when you think about it. Rob's usually impatient with any affectation or pretence. We thought he tolerated Graham out of pity though that's not in character either. What are you getting at? He could easily have avoided Graham if he'd wanted to.'

'Maybe he couldn't. Maybe Graham knew about the drugs conviction, or worse...'

Frank turned the wheel that controlled the angle of his backrest as he interrupted her. 'It was Rob who questioned the coroner's verdict, asked you to challenge it. Why would he want you to poke your nose into a crime he'd committed and got away with?'

'But he only came to me after Benny had said the force wasn't satisfied and that several officers, himself including, intended to take it further if they could. He was supposed to be Graham's friend. He had to appear to support an attempt to find out exactly what happened to him, to line up on the right side.'

Frank was sitting bolt upright. Now that she had his undivided attention, she willed him to disprove and dismiss her arguments. 'The drugs story keeps turning up from different sources. I suspect they came through Leon. He wriggled out a few years ago when his mates were rounded up and I think he's carried on their business. He's offered pills—through his minions—to Peter Crowther. Linda says Graham went to tackle him about it.'

'That's something else that sounds out of character. Anyway, I thought what Linda said was off limits.'

Zoe shrugged, knowing she was being inconsistent. 'Peter says his father went in for moral blackmail. Leon told Graham drugs were readily available and that Rob was implicated.'

Frank was visibly upset. 'Using, you mean, or supplying? You mean Graham was blackmailing Rob? It wouldn't be any good. He couldn't afford to pay.'

Zoe blinked. She had not considered a financial aspect. 'I mean Rob had to put up with Graham's unwanted company, friendship even, in exchange for his silence. It would explain why he took the carrier-bag from Graham's locker. Maybe Benny's accusation that he'd taken something from it that implicated himself wasn't far from the mark. It was a senseless thing to do for the reasons he gave. No! Forget all that. If Rob could get into Graham's locker, he'd have removed anything incriminating long ago.'

'But he couldn't. Most of the lockers don't lock. A few people, including Graham, provided their own padlocks.'

'So how did he manage it on the Sunday Graham died?'

'Took the key from Graham's pocket whilst they waited for the police to arrive?

He was alone with the body whilst Ken Hammond was taking the two youngsters home.'

'Or after he'd made sure Graham was dead and before anyone had come along to find him.'

The lights of a variety of riverside buildings were reflected on the surface of the Thames. Zoe thought, not for the first time, that the Royal Festival Hall was an entirely suitable and satisfactory setting for the enjoyment of music. Cosy inside the restaurant, she and Frank drank tea and admired the scene through huge areas of plate glass in the wall.

A little while later, she felt almost ill with excitement as she took her place in the auditorium. Nothing would ever make her blasé about great music performed by great artists. It projected her immediately into a state she could not describe, exalted, translated to something more than her everyday self, capable of an enjoyment denied to ordinary mortals, the sort that would, perhaps, be the unending reward of the faithful in the next life.

Zoe's theology was mystic, undefined. Vague and muddled, according to the Reverend Wayne Chester. None the less, it was real and vivid. It included the tenet that great music would inspire the constant worship that heaven seemed to demand and people on earth found so unappealing and difficult to sustain. Browning had tried to express what Zoe believed:

But God has a few of us whom he whispers
*   in the ear;*
The rest may reason and welcome; 'tis we
*   musicians know.*
...I feel for the common chord again,
The C Major of this life...

Once, at the age of fifteen or so, when such feats are easiest, she had learned 'Abt Vogler' by heart in its entirely. She was quite certain that she would meet Browning up in heaven when the time came.

Meanwhile, she fingered her programme and gazed around her and tried hard to keep in mind that she and Frank were here with a more practical purpose than hearing the concert. Since Jeffie had left Cloughton, Zoe had heard her sing chiefly on radio and compact discs. She had been increasingly impressed and expected the performance tonight to be thrilling. Just a tiny fraction of her mind hoped that she would be able to fault the voice 'in the flesh'. If it seduced her, she wouldn't have her wits about her.

Frank had taken his seat about a dozen

rows in front. It was early yet and less than a quarter of the stalls were filled. Zoe looked down again at the glossy booklet in her lap, examining the photographs of the singers and instrumental players who were to perform tonight and in the near future, then looked again at tonight's musical menu. Jeffie was to sing a wide-ranging programme, from 'O zittre Nicht, mein lieber Sohn' the coloratura aria of *Queen of the Night*, through lieder by Schubert, Mahler and Strauss to English folk-songs and a small group of Victorian drawing-room songs.

A glance through the printed words took Zoe back to her early childhood.

List for the breeze on wings serene
Thro' the light foliage sails.
Hidden amidst the forest green
Warble the nightingales.

She knew the song well. Just four short lines, but the deliciously tortuous interwoven arpeggios lasted for almost three minutes. She saw a succession of bygone family Christmases all rolled into one, her father on the piano stool, surrounded by both grandfathers and an assortment of uncles, roaring the stanza. Their wrinkled faces had writhed, their wide-open mouths revealed molars without benefit of dentist, but their beery breath had been beatified by the bliss with which they made music that was not contemptible.

Suddenly, Zoe was jerked back to the present. Someone was proceeding crab-like along row M and accosting Frank. Too far away to hear their conversation, she watched as each produced his ticket and Frank pointed to the seat in front of him. The young man appeared to be apologizing before making his side-stepping return journey to the aisle and claiming the seat that Frank had indicated. Maybe it was a genuine mistake but she continued to observe him until the lights dimmed.

Jeffie soon disappointed Zoe's hopes that she might be off form. She was a star, and the audience recognized her as such as soon as she had been a few moments on the stage. Mary Lister had been right in her view that the odd little seventeen-year-old had acquired a confident style of her own.

Zoe had expected formal evening dress and a straight-from-the-hairdresser coiffure for this prestigious occasion. Taller now, and slim as ever, Jeffie had her dark hair cropped close to her scalp, forming points in front of her ears and waxed to stand up, crew-cut fashion, on top of her head. She wore close-fitting pants and a collarless jacket in a glimmering silver fabric with a grey satin shirt and she held every eye.

Until the time came to go backstage as they had been invited, Zoe completely forgot that she had any purpose in the hall beyond appreciating what she was hearing. Then, following the route she had been given at the box office, she arrived safely outside Jeffie's dressing-room.

The door was opened by a man whom Zoe judged to be in his mid-forties. He was short and slight, but darkly handsome in a foreign sort of way. She was wondering quite what she meant by this unspoken phrase when Frank startled her by grasping the man's hand as they greeted one another with polite enthusiasm.

She noted thankfully, since it appeared he was to be included in the supper party, that the man was not in formal evening dress, so that their own elegant but all-day clothes would be suitable. She tried to think who he might be.

As Frank was performing the intro-ductions, it became obvious to Zoe that her chair would not go through the doorway of Jeffie's dressing-room. Her rescue was unexpected. Jeffie, totally unembarrassed, called out, 'I don't intend to make myself hoarse by shouting through to the corridor so you had better decide which of these two he-men is going to carry you inside.'

'He-man' seemed an unfitting description of Laurent Gilbert, who stood a good two inches shorter than his fiancée. Zoe committed her weight to Frank's proven biceps, whilst the Frenchman tucked the wheelchair closer to the corridor wall. Frank explained how he and Gilbert had become acquainted, first at the Cloughton concert and later at the Crossed Keys.

Zoe grinned. 'I bet he appreciated your conversation more than your singing. He isn't into lieder.'

Jeffie stuck a cushion unceremoniously into the small of Zoe's back, received the necklace with thanks and demanded, 'How's Aunty Mary? She always assures me she's flourishing and she's probably telling the truth.'

Zoe nodded. 'She expects to prosper and that makes it happen.' For a few moments, the two women reminisced, Zoe giving the required details of old schoolfriends and staff and such members of the chamber choir as had sung in the days when Jeffie belonged.

'Is that very good tenor still with you, the singing policeman?'

Zoe assured her that Jerry Hunter was still the backbone of the tenor line in both the church and chamber choirs when his duties allowed. 'The concert was bliss. It's so good to listen to a singer that you aren't a bit nervous for.'

Jeffie looked anxious rather than pleased. 'How was it really? I have to keep asking. It isn't conceit. We don't hear ourselves as other people hear us and we don't often find someone like you who's both informed and honest.'

'I can be both honest and reassuring. I heard every word. You don't seem to have several voices, like some singers, but the one voice has an amazing range of styles to fit the mood.'

Jeffie relaxed. 'It was very dry tonight. I had some moments though. Perhaps the critics will be kind. I suppose *they're* mostly informed and honest.'

'Cocky and rudely outspoken, you mean.' Laurent spoke ruefully as he dispensed sherry.

Jeffie disposed of half the contents of her glass in one gulp, then replaced it on the tray and abandoned it. 'What did you think of the programme?'

'Wonderful, except for the *Queen of the Night.*'

'Did I make a hash of it?'

Zoe shook her head. 'No, all the fireworks were there. I just don't like pieces that are written to show off vocal gymnastics.'

'Neither do I, but Masterman was in one of the boxes. I'm hoping he might take me on, and top notes mean money on the opera stage.'

'I've heard Zoe's uncles singing some of those notes you finished with.'

Zoe smiled at Frank, appreciating his effort to join in a conversation where he felt out of his depth. 'I love those nineteenth- and early twentieth-century drawing-room songs. I wondered how they'd sound as solos, without their close harmonies, but the ridiculous, over-elaborated cadenzas compensated and kept the right atmosphere,' she said.

Jeffie nodded. 'And the drifting into the minor when the words are on the melancholy side—which they usually are. They're comfortable to finish with when your voice is getting tired, and most people have a sneaking weakness for them because their grandparents used to sing them—even snobs who cross you off their list of serious performers when they learn that you're aware of which pop songs are in the Top Ten.'

Jeffie declared herself ready to depart for the wine bar where their supper had been reserved. Zoe was amused to see that the preparation of her person had consisted of merely removing all her make-up and replacing the satin shirt and silver jacket with a scarlet polo-necked sweater over the silver pants.

At supper, the conversation continued to be musical but Zoe was thankful on Frank's behalf that it now consisted of amusing anecdotes. Laurent described the rage of a prima donna of his acquaintance, whose reviews had, in an endeavour to be complimentary, described her as 'succulent'. At one point, Frank found an opening to enquire of their hostess her opinion of the artistry of Tina Turner. Zoe knew she would stand or fall in his estimation according to her reply.

When the meal was ended and the conversation had moved round to the merits and demerits of various singing teachers, Laurent realized that Frank had had his fill of musical theory and gossip and bore him off to the bar. Relieved of the burden of monitoring his mood and drawing him into the conversation, Zoe let Jeffie have her head.

She demanded Zoe's opinion of her concert outfit but went on, before it could be offered, 'People are paying to look at you as well as to listen. You can't help your basic face and shape, but Giovanni is very strict about getting the sound without any ugly contortions of your mouth and neck. And there's no excuse for not using clothes cleverly.'

'Aren't you afraid the audience might just be applauding the frock?'

Jeffie was not amused. 'I went to a recital by a young French girl the last time we went to visit Laurent's parents. It sounds silly, but I knew what her voice would be like as soon as I saw her. She wore dark, plum-coloured lipstick and a harsh royal-blue dress, and, sure enough, the voice was hard-toned and thin.' She paused to drink half a tumbler of water. 'There was a Spanish girl here a couple of weeks ago wearing a tight russet-brown suit. Sopranos shouldn't wear brown. It doesn't go with the sound.

'I usually try to dress to suit the programme, but it's difficult. In opera you're given no choice, of course, and in a good recital there's so much variety that you'd have to keep disappearing for quick changes if you were to suit the mood of each group of songs, so I just try to suit myself and my voice.

'Shall I order some more water?' Zoe shook her head. 'I have a pianist friend who chooses colours for composers. She says Beethoven is deep, rich red, Chopin is yellow for his brilliant style and grey for his tranquil mood. Britten is green...Laurent says she's mad. Of course, the lines of a dress are important too. Not many composers can take frills.'

207

'Not many singers' figures can either.' Zoe's attention began to wander. Snatches of Jeffie's monologue floated round her.

'...It's amazing, isn't it? The vocal chords are about half an inch long, and yet mine have ruled my life... It's not just the voice that's the gift. The passion is too. You can't work it up for yourself if it isn't there and you can't deny it if it is.' Zoe had no difficulty in agreeing with this.

She gathered that Jeffie was to take part in a prestigious singing competition later in the month. '...I don't like being entered for contests. If I'd wanted a competitive life I'd have joined a hockey team or something. I like it even less when I have to sing first. By the time the judges have heard the others they might not remember how good I was.'

Jeffie's current teacher was apparently keen on physical fitness. '...You can't rely just on your voice. You have to use your whole body to express yourself. By the time I have really learned how to sing, my voice will have worn out. You're one of the people I'll be relying on to tell me when that happens. In the meantime, I'm living according to Giovanni's rules on food and exercise and sleep. I'm thriving on his bullying. In a few minutes my taxi will pick me up so that I'll just manage to be in bed by midnight. You won't mind if abandon you to Laurent, will you?'

With perfect sincerity, Zoe assured her hostess that she would not mind at all.

When she rejoined the men in the bar, Zoe was relieved to find them roaring with laughter. Frank had obviously recovered his good humour. Perhaps he had been regaling Laurent with animal stories. The Frenchman rose politely to fetch orange juice for her. She watched his retreating back before she and Frank exchanged mock grimaces.

'She's full of herself, isn't she?'

'Not really. She's just high after the concert. She'll be different in the morning —not that we shall see her then. At least I enjoyed the music. Sorry about your evening—and we haven't found out anything new about Graham Crowther. I couldn't think of any way to introduce him into such conversation as there was.'

Frank looked smug. 'I did.'

'Clever.'

'No, I was just straightforward about it. Asked if the name meant anything to either of them. Not that it got me anywhere. He didn't react at all, though he did clear up one small mystery. It was Laurent who sent Graham the concert ticket. You know Graham was at the Cloughton concert that Laurent gave, the one you missed.

Afterwards, we were all in the pub together and Rob and I rescued Laurent from Graham's interminable ramblings about his unlikely past. He'd been claiming a great fondness for vocal music and never to have missed any of the concerts that Jeffie came back to give in Cloughton. Rob was startled because he'd never seen Graham at any of them.

'Laurent was glad to be rescued but he wanted to part from Graham on good terms, imagining him to be part of his fiancée's fan club. He did it by promising a complimentary ticket for her next London concert. It was as simple as that.'

'Nothing,' Zoe declared darkly, as they watched Laurent approaching with the orange juice, 'that has anything to do with the Crowther family is simple.'

Half an hour later, Laurent hopefully approached his fiancée's door. He observed that no light spilt through the crack between it and the floor. He tapped lightly, twice, and listened hard, then shrugged and crept respectfully away. Such devotion to her art.

Chapter Twelve

Having delivered a comatose Zoe back to her house on Sunday morning, Frank remained tactfully absent during most of the rest of the day. He was glad on his own account to sleep off the combined sufferings caused by Anne-Marie's party and Zoe's concert trip that had deprived him of two consecutive nights' sleep. He was more concerned, though, about the effects of the trip on Zoe's well-being. She had spent most of the previous day and night sitting down in the car, the concert hall and the restaurant. Now the dreaded pressure sores might raise their ugly heads.

Frank remembered her consultant's words of warning, soon after Zoe's accident. 'Blood is our lifeline. If the supply is cut off from part of the body by pressure, it will die.' It never happened to ordinary people, of course, since discomfort made them wriggle on to another area until the blood supply had been re-established. On just one occasion, the consultant's horror story had become a reality for Zoe. An innocent-looking area of red skin, when she continued to sit on it, had become bluish-red and had broken over a small area. Less vigilant than they should have been, they had left the small wound untreated. It had rapidly enlarged and become blue-black, obviously infected. Zoe's parents and Frank had been horrified and blamed themselves.

The consultant's stern words had offered small comfort. Left untreated for only a short while longer, the infection would have entered the bone and resulted in osteomyelitis. Zoe had accepted her hospitalization philosophically and had taken greater care ever afterwards. She was still inclined, however, to neglect the necessary precautions if she was denied the privacy that she wished for. The ultimate horror for her was to be labelled a hypochondriac. Now her GP, summoned in the morning by Zoe's mother, confined her to lying in bed until further notice. She submitted, unprotesting but furious.

Mitchell's Saturday was contrastingly hectic. Ginny's unborn baby having given her a bad morning, he had risen early and fed and watered his son and daughter before delivering them to his mother. He hoped the Santa they were to visit in Molloy's would not make too many rash promises which he would have to endeavour to keep. It was only the very beginning of December, so maybe by the twenty-fifth they might have forgotten about them. He knew, as he formed it, that this was a vain hope.

He planned to dash home to wield the vacuum cleaner and deal with the kitchen chaos. It would put him in Ginny's good books in the present circumstances. Sometimes, his endeavours on the domestic front were taken, as they were meant, as a gentle reminder that her housekeeping tended to the casual.

When he arrived, however, his doorstep was occupied by a sheepish-looking Rob Cameron. 'I thought I ought to... Well, it wasn't all my fault...but maybe I should have...'

His presence meant that he had made the first move in the reconciliation and Mitchell was prepared to be magnanimous. 'People tell me I make rather good coffee. Maybe we could dispense with the formalities and dispense Brazilian blend instead.' It was not often he managed a play on words and he departed for the kitchen, well pleased with himself.

'Zeugma!' announced a voice from the bottom of the stairs. Virginia had recovered and begun her day.

'What?'

'What you've just done. Used the same

213

word in two senses. You're coming on, Benny. You'll be writing poetry next.'

'Better things to do!' He spooned coffee-grounds into the filter-paper contempt-uously. Virginia grinned and went off to fill the washing-machine.

'I thought,' Mitchell remarked to Cam-eron as the coffee machine began to gurgle, 'we might go along and have a word with Mr Glasby tonight. I'm not prepared to tell him you're a policeman, but if that's what he chooses to think I shan't stop him.' Some twenty minutes later, the two men departed in high good humour to begin on their day's work.

They carried out Mitchell's plan, arriving at seven-thirty as Leon Glasby was adorning his person for a night on the town. He was not pleased to see them and wished that he had not just switched on the porch light, making it impossible to pretend to be out. He had evidently been right: the Morgan bitch was in cahoots with Bumptious Benny. She'd pay for it if he'd made his public confession for nothing.

He reviewed his situation in some alarm. Was it one of his exploits connected with the Blue Rose that Mitchell had stumbled on? It couldn't be anything arising out of what he'd told the *Clarion*. Even though illegitimate children were considered so

214

shocking in those days, he didn't think he had broken the law. Jeffie had been over sixteen at the time. There was no way she was going to blame him because she got mixed up with that old witch with the knitting needle and the gin or whatever she used. You couldn't be had up for giving advice—or for making threats, so long as there wasn't a witness.

He opened the door wide and essayed a charming smile that turned into a startled blinking as Mitchell's companion appeared beside him, dreadlocks dancing. Whatever sort of riff-raff was the police taking in these days?

He reassumed the smile. 'I'm always anxious to help the law, but if you keep me long you'll be causing a young lady to wait in the dark in a town centre that is rather rowdier than your colleagues should allow it to be.'

Mitchell stood impassively, enjoying Glasby's obvious unease. After several seconds he turned to Cameron. 'I always thought it was considered courteous to pick up a young lady from her home, but I don't have time to keep abreast of modern ways.' Cameron's hair jigged as he nodded. 'We'd like to have a look at your fishing-rod, Mr Glasby.'

Mystified, Glasby abandoned his mythical lady-friend. 'What for?'

'I've heard it's well worth a look. A Hardy, isn't it?'

Glasby shrugged. 'If you've heard so. I can't remember. You can do more than look. You can take it away with you if you like. I haven't used it in years.'

'There now, and I was saying if a person had paid in excess of a thousand pounds for a piece of equipment he wasn't likely to be willing to lend it.' Mitchell became suddenly serious. 'I suppose you didn't make this generous offer to someone else, about three weeks ago?'

Glasby shook his head and Mitchell was disappointed to realize that he believed the denial. 'Would you have noticed if someone had borrowed it without permission?'

Glasby hesitated, then shook his head again. 'I don't think I'd have missed it, but neither do I think I gave anyone the opportunity to poke around in my garage.'

'I'd be obliged if you'd allow *me* to poke around in it, to the extent of examining the rod.'

He agreed with ill-grace. 'As you please. If I refuse, you'll only go and get a piece of paper to make me.' He led the way, switched the lights on, glowered morosely as Mitchell made a thorough search and gave a curt nod when he availed himself of the permission already given to take the rod away. 'You've ruined my evening out. I may as well just watch television now.'

Mitchell smiled sweetly. 'Well, favour for favour. We'll pass on a message to that effect to any young woman we see hanging around in the precinct.'

'What? Oh, right.'

'By the way, does anyone else have a key to your garage?'

'No, but...' He hesitated, then went on, 'I lent it to someone a few months ago. He wanted me to store some bits and pieces for him that he didn't want his wife to see. He lost the key. I never had it back and I'm using the spare.'

'And the name of the someone?'

'Graham Crowther.'

Zoe had bitten the bullet and spent the whole day in bed. She had eaten without protest the high-protein diet, prescribed by her GP to promote healing and new flesh, and prepared by her mother (Zoe suspected) to reassert the control over her that the accident had given, and of which Zoe's increasing independence was now depriving her.

She was considerably cheered by the news that Mitchell and Cameron were on their way to visit her. When Frank had arrived too, they began a cautious exchange of information, Glasby's fishing-rod traded for Crowther's concert ticket. This completed, they fell silent, each busy with his or her own train of thought. Zoe's was exclusively concerned with how far she could trust Rob Cameron. She was the first to speak and it was to him.

'I shouldn't have thought Graham was a slapdash sort of man. He worked in a building society and was careful about canoeing safety. It doesn't seem likely that he would lose Leon's key.' She turned to Mitchell. 'Did you believe the key story?'

Mitchell nodded. 'Glasby was very much on the defensive at first. He obviously has a few guilty secrets that he thought we were on the track of, but when I concentrated on the fishing-rod I'm sure he was honestly puzzled. He was quite prepared to be helpful in that area because he had nothing to lose.'

Cameron, as soon as he could get a word in, declared, 'I couldn't see Graham losing anything, but I can quite easily see Linda pinching it.'

Zoe frowned. 'Did Linda know Leon? And how thick were he and Graham? Leon told me he had helped to get Helena into a part-time day-care place and that he'd taken Graham to the Blue Rose. Was he a blue-film type?'

Cameron shook his head vigorously.

'No, but he was the name-dropping type, and there are still some idiots in this town who are impressed when someone drops Glasby's. If Graham wanted to hang out with him, he'd have to go to the sleazy places where Glasby spends his time. As far as I know, Linda didn't socialize with him, though she must have known who he was and she probably met him as a friend of Graham's and over the arrangements for Helena.'

Another silence followed, full of furious thought, but the suggestions it threw up were all facetious. Mitchell summed up their rather negative conclusions impatiently. 'We're all convinced there's something that ties up Jeffie Lister, one or both of the Crowthers and Glasby, but we're just as far as ever from having any idea what it is. I don't think it's going to occur to us tonight. You might have had a restful day, Zoe, but ours has been long and hard and tomorrow will be the same.

Cameron and Mitchell departed and, when Frank showed signs of taking over Mrs Morgan's role of benevolent bully, he too was dispatched. Zoe used her shoulder muscles and the harness over her head to turn over on to her front. She shut her eyes and summoned up Linda in her imagination. The vision appeared, in the silver-grey funeral suit and, for some reason, the red polo-necked sweater that Jeffie had worn after the concert. Zoe was surprised. She had never seen Linda in red. She commanded her to take a stolen key, open up Leon's garage (having checked that he was out), remove his fishing-rod and use it in some way to drown her husband. The dream-Linda steadfastly refused to do any of these things.

Chapter Thirteen

Zoe would perhaps have been surprised to observe the resolution with which Linda Crowther rose at six o'clock the following day. The many necessary preparations for her journey would take more than an hour, but she hoped to reach the motorway ahead of the rush-hour. Since it was unlikely that she would meet anyone she knew, she dressed only with an eye to what was practical, pulling on jeans, sweater and short leather boots before rousing her daughter.

She stood for a moment in the bedroom doorway with the light switched on. A colourful frieze of nursery-rhyme characters ran round the apple-green walls at a child's eye level. Helena's favourite Humpty Dumpty was echoed in the design on the curtains and quilt. The floor covering was, of necessity, the tough, washable carpet designed for kitchens, but it was cheerfully checked in shades of green and cream. The bed and drawers were of pale pine and the effect of the combination of furnishings made the whole room attractive, marred only by its occupant.

Her fat face obliterated the lace-edged pillow. Her mouth hung open and she was snoring. It took a full thirty seconds of Linda's shaking to rouse her to consciousness. Linda sat her up, then drew back the curtain. Dim grey light filtered into their dim grey existence.

Linda heaved as she inspected Helena's protective pants before doggedly setting about the necessary washing and creaming. When the child squirmed and kicked, she administered a resounding slap on the leg, then regarded her fingermarks with grim satisfaction. She willed them to remain as evidence, till the resulting screams caused her to regret the punishment. She found she was screaming herself, 'Shut up! Shut up!'

Startled, the child sobbed quietly as Linda pulled on her clean underwear and covered it with her pink towelling dressing-gown. She distracted Helena with an elephant mobile—how appropriate—and dumped her in front of her dangle whilst she made her own breakfast, adding an egg to her usual toast. It was going to be a very long and very traumatic day.

Having fuelled herself satisfactorily, Linda set about making Helena's breakfast. Helena's life centred on food. Thank goodness for the dangle which had distracted her this long. She opened 'Helena's cupboard', then shut it again. Sod the cup that deposited its contents over her daughter's bibs and dresses! Sod the stupid dish with its rubber suction pads that Helena easily managed to unstick and overturn! The child had plenty of low cunning for the mayhem she loved to create, however stupid she was when you wanted her to co-operate.

Linda smiled grimly. Never mind; her days, maybe hours, of coping with Helena were numbered, so why not do things the easy way? She opened the drawer full of tea-towels and felt at the back where the bottle and powdered formula were hidden. Whilst the water boiled, she made the hole in the teat even bigger, then shovelled the powder into a jug, adding copious amounts of sugar. When the monster tasted that, she'd hopefully stop yelling for the chocolate Shreddies with which she loved to decorate the kitchen wall.

What wouldn't go into the bottle she'd pour into a vacuum flask for later. Helena was always less trouble fed than hungry. Better not to stuff her too full now, though. If the child threw up her lunch, it might just serve Linda's purpose, but breakfast must stay put. She couldn't have the car reeking for weeks.

Helena's eyes lit up at the sight of the bottle. She grabbed at it and stuffed the teat into her mouth. Linda wondered if she even remembered the times that Peter or Graham had patiently coaxed her to spoon food into her mouth whilst she screamed with frustration. She reactivated the dangle, swallowed her disgust at the sight of the glugging mouth, then went upstairs to fetch the child's clean top clothes.

By half-past seven Helena was buckled into her local-authority, extra-size baby car-seat, and her mother, snapped into her seat-belt, was leaving the driveway and heading for the M1.

The days were passing very slowly for Zoe. Frank decided on Tuesday that he would call round after supper to check up on her, but he would have to have an excuse ready. It was some time since he had overhauled her electric wheelchair. A Saturday job in a garage when he was a sixth-former had made him competent, and he regularly checked that the pulleys on the motor drive shafts had not worked loose and that the vertical bolt that located the motor mounting on the chair frame was in 'pinched tight' position, the locking nuts secure. That excuse would do nicely.

Having remained in bed, lying on her

front and listening to the radio, until tea-time, Zoe decided it was in the interests of her mental health to take a shower and find something useful to do. The wheelchair ought to be inspected, but she was still hoping that Frank might turn up and relieve her of this hated chore. Since he took such pleasure in tinkering with it, she felt no guilt at the small self-indulgence of leaving it to him.

As she wondered whether she should begin, the telephone rang. Glad of the reprieve, she picked up the receiver.

'I'm so sorry to disturb your evening.' But Peter Crowther sounded more worried than apologetic. Zoe assured him that she had spent a lazy day alone and was glad of the distraction. 'It's just that I can't seem to contact my mother. I always ring home at some point on a Monday. Yesterday, I tried ringing at nine in the morning because I was going to be busy later. There was no answer then. I tried again mid-morning, then lunch-time, tea-time and about nine in the evening, and still there was no reply.

'Wherever Mum had been, I thought she'd be certain to be back by then because of Helena's bedtime. Besides, she hardly ever takes her far from home. I've had no luck all day today either. I've tried both grans and her posh friend, Mrs Groves.

We all talked as though there were heaps of people Mum might have gone to see, but we all know really that she hasn't any close friends, certainly not anyone she'd take Helena to spend the night with.'

Zoe was needled. 'None of you knows that. And you're a big boy now. You don't think she should miss the chance of a trip out just because she might receive a casual phone call from you? Maybe Helena's playgroup has organized an expedition.'

'Wouldn't the grans know about it?'

'Not necessarily. They're not surprised or anxious are they?'

'Surprised, yes. I suppose they didn't seem very worried, though. Grannie Crowther said it was a good sign and Grandma Kelsey said it was time Helena had a change from the usual four walls and that Mum should have taken her out before.'

'Has the car gone?'

'I don't like to cross-question the neighbours. Mum would be furious.'

Zoe sighed. 'Give me your number. I'll make a few enquiries and get back to you when I know something. If she's staying with someone, though, it may be a day or two before I hear.'

Peter thanked her but seemed reluctant to hang up. 'I just wondered if...well, if she'd been arrested.'

'Stop looking for trouble, Peter. That was only a theory of yours. You don't know she's been stealing.'

'I do, but you're right that I can't prove it.' This time he did ring off.

In spite of the reassuring scolding she had given Peter, Zoe was seriously worried. She was fairly sure that Linda would not have taken a trip out for her daughter's benefit, certainly not an overnight one. The grandparents were the obvious people to have been left in charge of Helena if Linda had gone off on a trip of her own. What if she'd been wrong all along the line? What if Linda had first disposed of Graham, against whom she had the greater grudge, and had now gone off somewhere to kill Helena?

It wouldn't be difficult. Down's children had breathing problems and would be very easy to suffocate. They were greedy and trusting so it would be a simple matter to administer poison. They didn't understand danger. It would be all too easy to stage an accident. Zoe became anxious for Frank to arrive.

In anticipation and to keep her hands busy, Zoe went into the kitchen, opened a tin of tuna fish and began to make a huge pile of sandwiches. She realized that she was hungry. She had slept through lunch-time and woken during the early afternoon still sated from the huge meal they had eaten the previous evening and distracted by a radio performance of Dvořák's 'Stabat Mater'. The performance had cheered her because the Cloughton Chamber Choir's efforts seemed not to compare badly with the BBC Northern Singers', which had been received by the studio audience with rapturous applause.

She divided the fish virtuously, mixing only Frank's half with mayonnaise. She would ring him as soon as she had finished the plateful and tell him that, according to her Cordon Bleu Cookbook, the life of a sandwich was a mere twenty minutes.

Thus summoned, Frank arrived in ten and dispatched the contents of his plate with a celerity that suggested that he too had missed his lunch. He was in masterful mood and ordained that she should lie on the couch whilst he fiddled with the chair.

He disappeared to the garage and, obediently supine, she mentally rehearsed her last session with Linda Crowther. At first, Linda had not wanted to talk about her daughter at all. That was to be expected if she was planning to get rid of her. Zoe had suggested that antagonistic feelings towards the child were permissible and her implied invitation had opened up the floodgates on Linda's frustration and resentment.

If she had read Linda aright, this should have helped to alleviate the desperation that might have led her actually to harm the child. But, maybe she'd read her quite wrongly. What if, having drowned her husband, she was finding it much easier to contemplate killing Helena, and restoring her freedom of choice, her power to control her own life.

Throughout the interview, Linda's resentment and suspicion of other people's sympathy had been much to the fore, yet only by accepting help was there any way that she could manage. Linda was not stupid. She had observed the 'old' look of other carers. Looking back and looking forward, she saw herself for ever being used by others. She knew she needed to wrest her life back for herself.

But could someone who had married a man she didn't love because it would have been impolite to refuse him ever learn to be firm and reasonable in asserting her rights? Zoe thought not. Linda would endure till she cracked and then, more than likely, she would lose all control.

What a pity that she and Graham had not been able to weep together, struggle together, maybe even triumph together over Helena's development. Linda imagined the rest of the world condemning her for Helena, judging her performance as a mother. Her upbringing had made her see life as a competition. She had to impress the judges, who were all the other people she met. Graham could not have helped her there. Such an attitude to life would have made no sense to him.

The bleak phrases Linda had used ran through Zoe's mind: '...how permanent the difficulties...medication wouldn't help, or minor surgery...if we had been a proper family...the clumsy, monotonous tedium of her company...' The hollow-toned hopelessness had made a deep impression on Zoe, fixed the phrases in her mind. What option had someone caught in such a downward spiral but desperate rebellion? Maybe it was too late to do anything already. Maybe the child was dead even now.'

'Frank!' Zoe's panic-stricken yell brought Frank scampering from the garage.

Linda's Monday had not gone entirely to plan. Far from being a help, Helena seemed to frustrate all her plans to be apprehended. The two of them had not arrived in Birmingham until half-past eleven after two stops to change trainer pants, and a third on the hard shoulder of the motorway when Helena's screaming had brought Linda to a point where she was incapable of driving on.

She had been able to find nothing that might be troubling the child. Desperately, she had offered biscuits, toys and stern warnings in turn. Finally, in a fit of rage that rivalled her daughter's, she had slapped the puffy red face. Helena had screamed on until she had fallen asleep, exhausted. As the child's flush of temper receded, Linda saw her own livid fingermarks picked out on the fat cheeks. She drove on, unrepentant.

Setting to work as soon as she had found a parking spot and transferred Helena to a pushchair, Linda trundled it into the first branch of Marks and Spencer's that she saw. She noted with approval the two uniformed security men who stood in the main entrance, greeting each customer with a hostile glare. She walked round, blatantly stuffing a miscellany of merchandise on to the tray beneath the pram body before wheeling it past the security point and out of the store.

No one followed. No one accosted her. Staff and customers alike had averted their eyes from the pram and its dribbling, incoherently babbling passenger. No one wanted to become involved with them. When she finally succeeded in getting Helena taken into care, such people would criticize her. After all, if the mother of such a monster refused to take full responsibility for it, then they themselves might be peripherally touched by its existence. Their message came through loud and clear: people like Helena should not be brought into shops where normal people had to make their purchases, to embarrass and upset them.

Linda moved on to the next store and came out with unwrapped goods completely filling the space between the tray and the body of the pram. Helena, fascinated by her mother's activities, beamed and jabbered. Soon, though, she would become hungry.

Linda made her way back to the carpark, filled the boot with her unwanted acquisitions, poured the contents of the vacuum flask into the feeding-bottle and handed it to the child. It was cold, but she had no energy to spare to lift fifty pounds of limp, flaccid flesh back into the car and then out again when the bottle was empty. Nor could she be bothered to investigate the state of Helena's pants.

She ate a banana and a chocolate biscuit herself before making her way back to the city centre. As she was leaving Debenham's, half an hour later, she paused on the mat that activated the automatic doors and looked behind her. There was no one within three or four yards of her, certainly no one near enough to follow her outside and accost her before she was swallowed up in the crowds on the pavement.

With a sigh, Linda moved over to a chair, left for the convenience of the old and the infirm, and unloaded on to it a basket of dried flowers, two outsize shirts, a bottle of body lotion and a hideous pottery dog, priced in three figures. Sadly, she pushed the pram with its empty tray out into the street.

Trudging past further expanses of plate glass that protected displays of kitchenware, then toys, she came to a door and pushed the pram through it without raising her eyes. Thus it was that, when a rather more vigilant security officer finally followed and stopped her, Linda was unaware of which retail business was her accuser.

She accompanied the officer without comment back through the store, through a door marked 'Staff Only' and thence into a lift which bore the three of them and the pram to a small office in the upper regions. Sitting on the chair provided, she watched in silence as her spoils were lifted from the tray and placed on the office desk. Helena too stared in unblinking quiet at the motley array of goods till the last item was in place. It was a clown doll and she babbled and reached out for it.

After a slight hesitation, the woman

233

behind the desk gave a nod and the security officer held out the doll towards the pram before Helena had worked up enough steam for a full-throated roar. Linda replied briefly to polite questions. No, she had paid for none of the goods and had no receipts. Yes, she did understand what she had done. Yes, she did know that it was the shop's policy to prosecute all thieves. No, she did not require anything for the child before the police arrived.

They arrived in the form of a diminutive, rosy-faced blonde who tickled Helena and made her laugh before formally arresting Linda and summoning a squad car. Linda was sure that the attention to her daughter had been to enable the young WPC to examine the mark on her face that had reappeared in the stuffy heat of the shop.

Obeying the instructions she was given, she followed the constable out of the office, back into the lift and out through the shop to the car, walking easily, head unbowed. She knew no one in Birmingham. The good or bad opinion of total strangers was of no importance to her. She would be quite happy to come back here for the court case and no one in Cloughton would be any the wiser, except for the people for whose benefit the whole charade was being played out.

She omitted to tell the constable or her

colleagues in the car that Helena needed to be restrained in her special seat whilst being driven. The police were in charge now, of both herself and her daughter. Any harm that came to either of them would not be her responsibility.

As it happened, the short journey across the city was accomplished quite safely and she wheeled Helena into the police station with continued equanimity. She would submit with quiet dignity to the procedures that aimed at disarming and humiliating her. She would bear in mind that she, Linda, was in charge of this affair. She had worked hard to get here. These officers were being manipulated into her plan.

Having thus encouraged herself, she submitted to the perfunctory patting of her contours and placed the contents of her pockets on to the station sergeant's desk: a grubby handkerchief, Helena's Smarties, a rain-hood. She explained that she carried no handbag, but handed over the large bag clipped to the pram handle that contained all that was necessary for Helena. She handed over her daughter too, deducing with grim satisfaction from the smell that her pants were in their usual disgusting state.

Two officers supervised the business of her own admittance into custody, talking to each other as if she could not hear them. As a photographer took three shots, two profiles and one full-face, and her fingers were rolled in turn on the ink-pad and pressed on white paper, she learned from their reciprocal mutterings that her name had been tapped into their computer to check whether she had previous convictions, any record of violence, any mention on a drugs register.

Then a female officer began to question her, curt but not hostile. 'Name?'

'You already have it.'

'Address?' When Linda gave it, the officer showed a spark of interest. 'You're a long way from home. What are you doing in Birmingham?'

Linda shrugged, not sure what answer would be the most advantageous to her cause. 'Shop-lifting.'

The officer called over a colleague and consulted with him. His questions were considerably more aggressive. 'What proof can you give us that you live at this address?'

'What kind of proof do you want?'

The WPC was more placatory. 'We need to know that you haven't given us a false name and address. It's unusual for a woman not to carry a handbag with identifying documents and all the personal things you might need for yourself.'

Linda scowled. 'If you'd ever travelled

with a Down's child, you'd know you have quite enough of a burden carrying the things you need for her.'

The male officer cut in abruptly. 'What are the neighbours called on either side of you?' With sinking heart, Linda gave the names. She had not anticipated this. 'What colour are your front-bedroom curtains?'

'Sage green. How can you check on that?'

'*We* ask the questions.' Why did he need to be so rude? She had stolen from the shop, not from him. She was helping to keep him in a job. She turned away from him and addressed everything else she had to say to the female officer. The young woman helped her to make a statement that made much of her husband's death and the trials of caring for Helena single-handed. The policewoman's version was much more of a bid for sympathy than Linda would ever have brought herself to make on her own behalf. The effect of her story was being enhanced by Helena's screams in the background as the officer who had taken charge of her failed to pacify her.

Linda wondered whether to mention her previous offences. It would emphasize her own mental deterioration and the possibility of Helena's moral corruption, but she was not sure if the offences committed in Cloughton could be dealt with by Birmingham magistrates. She should never have begun stealing in Cloughton. She had had the idea of coming so far from home too late. Now, she could end up facing Georgina Groves across a courtroom as she pursued her magisterial duties. Perhaps she would have a chance to talk to a solicitor later, or to her social worker when she got back home. The woman hadn't done anything very useful so far. This would give her her chance.

Linda read the statement through and signed it. 'Where's your colleague gone?'

'I'm afraid he's organizing a search of your car...'

'I *told* you about all the stuff in the boot!'

'...and of your house. When your proper address has been established and the search of your house has been made by an officer from your local force, you'll be given police bail. That means you'll sign a document promising to return on the date given for your hearing.' The officer became aware of Linda's panic. 'It's better if we get everything from you before we find out for ourselves. Is there anything else you want to tell me?'

Linda sat still and closed her eyes but her inner turmoil continued. 'Yes. I'm going to be sick.'

Chapter Fourteen

Detective Sergeant Hunter, the 'singing policeman', was disgruntled. Having been commandeered for overtime, he was having to spend it on tedious paperwork. It would still be there when his regular shift began, and nothing seemed particularly urgent. Late afternoons, when the children were at home, were precious. It wouldn't be long before Tim and Fliss would be leaving home altogether, and William would soon have passed through the delightful toddler stage and he would have missed it.

He was not displeased to be summoned by his DCI. He hoped something more interesting had come up. The file the chief inspector was reading when he went in seemed to contain very little. He closed it and Hunter saw Graham Crowther's name. 'I thought that was closed.'

His DCI grinned. 'Fresh evidence is the key that reopens them.'

'So, what's come up?'

'Sweet FA, but there might be a chance to find something.' Hunter listened carefully whilst Linda Crowther's predicament was explained to him. 'Two

239

uniformed men are on their way round there now, to search for stolen property and to check on the neighbours. I'm sure they'd appreciate a helping hand. I don't know what I'm hoping you'll come up with. Just sniff around a bit and hope something interesting presents itself.'

Hunter whistled the tenor line of the previous Sunday's anthem as he made for the car-park. So, Browne hadn't been any happier than the rest of them at having to abandon their enquiries into Crowther's death. He should have known, given the old man a bit of credit.

Hunter found the house with no difficulty and examined it from the shelter of his car. The garden was basically well cared for, though the path and small lawn were marred by patches of sodden, unswept leaves. It looked as if its usual meticulous carer had been away for a short while. He supposed, in one sense, this was precisely the case. At least the paintwork was clean and the curtains fresh. He rapped on the door, found it unlocked and went in.

The uniformed constable who was checking the contents of a kitchen unit rose from his knees. 'Blimey, what's going on? We can manage a search for stolen goods without an army of CID to supervise.'

240

'Who else is here?' Before he received an answer, the shout of laughter from the nether regions told him it was Mitchell. *You're* looking for anything that's obviously stolen. I'm sure you're more than competent. *We're* here—hoping you'll keep your mouths shut about us—using the opportunity to look for anything that will give us a chance to reopen a case.'

'The Crowther drowning?'

Hunter nodded and the constable hurried off to impart the news to his colleague. Hunter found Mitchell in the hall. 'I suppose your antennae told you we were all here. You wouldn't by any chance be in league with Zoe Morgan?'

'Why should you think that?' Mitchell was not good at injured innocence.

'A week or two back, she asked me to have a word with her after church. When I went to find her, her excuse for detaining me was so feeble that I knew she'd been going to say something else and had changed her mind. Then, later and elaborately casually, she asked if I'd met any of her new canoeing friends on the day we spent on the Crowther case.'

'She'd probably decided in the meantime that she'd be better off trying to worm everything out of me.'

This theory was both likely and irritating and Hunter ignored it. As Mitchell's

241

superior, he banished him upstairs whilst he tackled the living-rooms himself. 'We'll wander independently for half an hour and then compare notes.' He marched back to the kitchen.

There were no dirty dishes and everything had been tidily put away. Chairs and carpets were stained from spills. There were photographs of three generations of the family, expensively framed, and beautiful small ornaments. Several exquisite small water-colours of wild flowers were ranged along one wall. The dresser contained good cutlery and embroidered linen table-cloths and napkins. The carpet, though, was cheap and worn.

Though the downstairs rooms were well cared for they were somehow bleak. Their different features were mismatched. It was not so much the colours—there was no need for the colours in a room to match—but there was no impression of a united couple building up a home together. There was not even an impression of two different personalities. Hunter supposed that, like beggars, thieves had their choices restricted by what was on display and discreetly portable.

Mitchell, meanwhile, was pottering happily round the bedroom. In contrast with the elegant garments in Linda's wardrobe, her pyjamas, folded on her pillow, were of unappealing winceyette. A snub to her husband, or a protection when she had to get up on chilly nights to attend to a handicapped child? He decided on the former, after he had examined the underwear in the drawers. And, of course, the marriage had needed benefit of counselling and Linda had shown few signs of grief. Ginny's outer garments were much more casual than Linda's but he was glad she never wore knickers like these underneath.

At the end of the stipulated half-hour, the four officers conferred. The evidence that Linda Crowther had been stealing for some time was convincing to them but there was not much that was likely to lead to a prosecution.

'She was like a magpie,' one of the constables remarked.

Mitchell agreed. 'The stealing wasn't motivated by need, or even greed—not normal greed, anyway. Who needs twenty-one blouses and seventeen pairs of shoes or fourteen jackets? There isn't much jewellery. That's usually well guarded, of course.'

'The child's clothes are as pretty and plentiful as her own,' Hunter observed, 'but there's precious little for her to play with.' He looked up from his notebook. 'Petty thieving is an inadequate term for this sort

243

of wholesale helping herself. Maybe the sheer amount of it, plus the Birmingham offences, will swing it in court. Any fool can work out what's been going on.'

Having carried out their instructions, the uniformed officers left. Hunter, to Mitchell's surprise, settled himself into a chair. 'Mrs C can't leave Birmingham until those two have telephoned the all-clear. That leaves us another three hours at the very least.' Mitchell grinned to himself. Hunter had at long last learned what he himself had known by instinct from the beginning: you seldom got results without breaking the rules.

Together they set about an examination of the papers in the drawers of the desk in the hall. The interesting one turned up in Hunter's pile. 'I'm sure this wasn't there when we looked before. We'll have to compare the handwriting.' He handed over the note that Graham Crowther had left for his wife on the Sunday morning of his death.

Mitchell read it eagerly, surprised that it had ever existed except in Linda's story, and even more surprised by what it said.

After hot, sweet police tea, Linda's panic abated and she began to feel better. What a police search of her house suggested to the local officers would be very difficult

244

for them to prove. All the incriminating labels had been removed from what she had taken, even before she left the shops she had stolen them from.

She heaved a great sigh of relief. The ordeal was over—for now at any rate. She deserved a treat and she could afford it. Her small savings could be spent because the insurance money was on its way. She would stay overnight in Birmingham and leave the horrendous journey home until tomorrow. She considered the practical problems of the scheme. Her clothes were not suitable for dinner in a hotel restaurant.

She'd bath Helena and get her safely off to sleep, then ask for a tray meal and a bottle to be sent up to her room. After her hysterics at the police station, the child was beginning to look very sleepy. She'd better hurry. A short nap in the pushchair or the car just before bedtime had been known to set her up till midnight. Linda had seen a small, respectable-looking establishment round the corner from the police station and she made her way there.

She had not meant to deceive the hotel receptionist, but the pram-hood was pulled up against the slight drizzle, and, as she approached the high counter to book in, the pram was hidden from view. The girl became aware of Helena's condition only after all the arrangements had been made. Linda suspected that, if the child had drawn attention to herself with her usual grizzling as they had come in, the receptionist would have 'regretted' that no room was available.

She explored the one they had been allocated with satisfaction. Nasty plastic furniture—imitation teak—that Helena couldn't harm, a television set with a twenty-six-inch screen and Teletext, coffee-making facilities. It would do. The decoration was unpleasing, but once Helena was in bed she could turn out the central light and the glow from the pink-shaded lamp would be cosy. The armchairs were good-quality and blissfully comfortable.

It was a pity she had packed no toys but at least she had the dangle. She attached it to a chest of drawers, set it in motion and went to run the child's bath. She saw, as she undressed her daughter, that all the slap marks had disappeared. They had been fading fast, even as the constable had examined them. They had been made by striking in anger and she had found herself unable to renew the evidence in cold blood. Whether this was because of a modicum of affection for the child, or because of her usual inability to act, she refused to contemplate. The police questions about her feelings for her daughter had given her reason for optimism.

She prolonged the bathtime and entertained the child until she could bear the tedium no longer, then dropped her, exhausted, into one of the twin beds. She should stay there till morning. The mouth fell reassuringly open and the irritating snuffling and snorting began almost immediately. Linda switched on the kettle, grimaced at the sachets of powdered creamer, made instant black coffee and sat down to review her situation. Whatever the police believed had happened to Graham, thankfully no one seemed to have thought of accusing her, and the award from the insurance company, though tardy, seemed certain to arrive. It wouldn't keep her for ever but it would certainly allow her a breathing-space to decide what she wanted to do.

She smiled to herself. Her chief talent seemed to be for stealing. It was certainly a lucrative career, but she had found she enjoyed it for its own sake. The risks were exciting, and it had provided her with a way of getting even with life for treating her so shabbily. After the court case that would result in having Helena taken away from her, she would have to keep a low profile for a while, as she might be watched. She wondered if she had done enough to ensure that the authorities would consider her an unstable and unsuitable parent for a handicapped child.

She hoped so. She didn't want to have to resort to an overdose. Not being a chemist, she would find it difficult to be drastic enough to be taken seriously without actually putting her life in danger. Linda drained her cup, reached for the telephone and made her request for supper in her room.

The girl's voice was chilly. This was a small establishment with a small staff. Food was served only in the dining-room.

Linda apologized. 'It's just that my little girl's a Down's child. You saw her in the foyer when I booked in. She might cause a disturbance in the dining-room and I wanted to avoid that.' Linda smiled grimly as the refusal was immediately withdrawn. Five minutes later a loaded tray was brought in.

She took an inventory. Smoked-salmon sandwiches for her, cream cheese for her daughter. She supposed they wouldn't know Helena would spit them out as soon as she found they weren't sweet. She picked up a vacuum flask, unscrewed the top and sniffed freshly ground coffee. A scrap of paper attached to the bottle of white wine informed her that it came with the compliments of the management. There was a chocolate sandwich cake which was more in Helena's line and, finally, on the other side, a litre carton of fresh milk and several individual packets of breakfast cereal. So, Helena was not to upset their breakfast clientele either. She would have to see about that. She dismissed, without a tip, the boy whose eyes were riveted on her snoring daughter and settled down to her meal, alone with her thoughts.

She was out on bail, which was just what she had expected, except that police bail seemed to mean something different from what she had understood. She had expected to have to name some person who could be persuaded to offer a financial guarantee of her appearing in court. She had been hesitating between an appeal to her GP and her social worker, wondering whether either would have responded to her plea. For a few moments, she had even considered applying to Zoe Morgan.

She was glad that none of it had been necessary. Zoe in particular would have refused to be manipulated. She had meant her sessions with Zoe to be part of her scheme to be rid of her daughter. A Relate counsellor's report of an unhappy, unstable marriage would strengthen Linda's argument. Somewhere along the line, though—pretty well from the beginning, in fact—Zoe had turned the tables on her and she had found herself telling the truth about herself, her life and her marriage, at least in so far as she dared to reveal it.

She uncorked the wine. A corkscrew had been provided but no glass. Perhaps 'the management' expected the members of a Mongol's family all to drink out of unbreakable plastic beakers. She reached for the tooth-mug. It wouldn't alter the taste, and they had sent rather a good Chardonnay.

Screwing up and tucking into her pocket the note tied to the bottle-neck recalled her similar action when she had found the note Grahamn had left on the table for her on his last day. She could smile now at Graham's funny little ways. She was glad that she had not allowed the police to see, in writing, his last pathetic lie. She had genuinely mislaid the note at first. Now it lay, carefully smoothed out, in the desk drawer in the hall.

She would never marry again. She should never have done so in the first place. Talking so intimately to Zoe had helped her to realize that. The deluge of complaint Zoe had listened to so patiently wasn't because Graham was a bad husband but because she needed to live alone. That was why, by one means or another, she must now get rid of Helena.

By dint of being rather less than polite to her mother over the telephone, Zoe fended off a further day of supervision and force-feeding. She was rather ashamed of herself as she replaced the receiver, and by lunchtime she would have been glad of anyone's company. The fact that it was Laura Gibson who presented herself was a bonus. 'My clients cancelled,' she announced, breezily. 'We were all concerned about you, so I was elected to come and represent everyone. How are you?'

Zoe grimaced. 'Mending fast, thank you. My temper, in inverse proportion, is getting more ragged. You're a godsend but can you make your own coffee? What's the gossip?'

'Yes, if you tell me where to find everything, and you are because you're wearing your ring again. What happened?'

Zoe grinned. 'I met the wheelchair-bound counsellor I was looking for and she talked some sense into me.' She described the tea party with Mary Lister until the coffee cups were empty and the takeaway pizzas that Laura had brought were eaten. Zoe had munched happily and made no mention of her diet.

As they both wiped greasy fingers, Laura

asked, 'What do you want to do about Linda on Friday? Will she be coming? I've transferred the Smiths to my own list for this week and I've taken it upon myself to cancel your other appointments until further notice, but I know Linda is special for you. Shall I take her on too, or shall I put her off till you're back?'

Zoe shook her head. 'I might be able to get in by Friday. I really don't want to let her down.' She related, briefly, the news of Linda's brush with the law that she had received in a call from Mitchell.

Laura was concerned. 'Do you think she'll talk to you about it?'

Zoe laughed. 'I can't decide whether she'll totally deny it or give it to me blow by blow in the minutest detail. It won't be anything in between.'

'How's it going?'

Zoe sighed. 'I wish so much that Graham had attended that first session. I could understand a lot more if I'd had a chance to hear his side.'

'What would you have asked him?'

'Well, first of all, why he married her. I'm not sure that I believe in marriages made in heaven, but I can't believe that one partner can be genuinely and satisfactorily in love if the other isn't. Surely, if love isn't mutual, it's only an illusion.'

Laura shrugged and rearranged herself

more comfortably in her armchair. 'I can't get philosophical when I'm full of pizza.'

Zoe was not to be put off. 'The trouble is, she was pretending so successfully to be someone else that Graham was fooled and at least became infatuated with the image she was projecting. The marriage couldn't work because she wasn't what he needed or what she appeared to be. The illusion wasn't any use to him. She wasn't there for him, to use a trendy expression that I'm not very fond of.'

'Have you found out why she pretends?'

'I didn't need to. She's perfectly clear about it. Rightly or wrongly, she believed her mother loved her only in proportion to how thoughtful, obliging and well mannered she was. She learned the code of acceptable behaviour and, underneath, she understood nothing of the needs of all the people she was being nice to. She just said yes to all their demands, including Graham's proposal of marriage.

'She couldn't keep it up twenty-four hours a day for ever though. When the pretence broke down there was nothing left but resentment on both sides.'

'So, what are you trying to achieve now?'

'I'm trying to get through to her that she's the only one who can change things. That it's no use latching on to people like her GP to make the disobliging refusals that she finds so difficult on her behalf.' She abandoned her earnest tone. 'Shall we compound our greed? There's an apple crumble in the fridge that my mother made...'

Laura rose obediently to get it out and placed it in the microwave oven whilst she made custard. As they were greedily spooning it into their mouths, Laura asked, somewhat indistinctly, 'So, where does the stealing fit in?'

Zoe shook her head. 'I don't quite know, unless she's missing the security that she didn't realize Graham was giving her. Though from what Benny says it's been going on since long before he died...'

The conversation passed to more trivial matters, but, after Laura had taken her leave, Zoe continued to concentrate on Graham Crowther. So much depended on what sort of man he had been. Unfortunately for her purpose, not only did the people who had known him disagree with each other about this, but the same people seemed to have seen him differently at different times.

Linda had painted a rather more sympathetic picture of him since she had been free, even for such a short time, from his stifling presence. The canoeists seemed sharply divided between those who found him contemptible and those who found him brave and sad. The intolerant Rob Cameron was at least sufficiently attached to him to want to see justice done over his death.

She dozed, and dreamed that Graham Crowther was being attacked by a fish. She woke and watched a television sleuth progress from finding an unidentified corpse to putting its killer behind bars within the space of half an hour. She watched the light fade from an angry red sky, and then another visitor made his way through the gloom. He had not known to collect her key from her mother's house down the road. She manoeuvred herself into her chair to let DS Hunter in, but he remained on the doorstep. 'I can't stay, I'm expected at home. I've brought you a message from Benny. He's been in court all day and he's doing a stint of overtime tonight. He thought you'd like to know it's because we've managed to get the Crowther file reopened. He says to tell you he'll be in touch.'

That same Wednesday morning, Linda Crowther was as glad to receive her visitor as Zoe had been. She had been wondering how to approach her social worker, wondering how annoyed she would be to receive an urgent appeal, how distracted from Linda's own problems she would be by the rest of her caseload. Now Mrs Holmes had made the first move and telephoned her. She would like to see Linda this morning if that was convenient. Linda was granting the interview instead of begging for it. Someone must have already told Mrs Holmes about the Birmingham affair.

Mrs Holmes would be worried about Helena. Would it be a good idea to have her daughter looking less immaculate than usual? She decided not. A few spills and stains would upset Linda herself more than it would trouble the rough and ready social worker. Should she offer tea, or would playing the competent hostess suggest that she was coping too well with her troubles? And how ought she to explain things?

Mrs Holmes was a much simpler soul than Zoe. A long, articulate justification of Linda's conduct would give her the impression that her client was still what she liked to call 'together'. It would be useful to be able to cry, to become hysterical. That was the kind of behaviour Mrs Holmes recognized as expressing distress. For Zoe's benefit, Linda had sacrificed her vanity and made sure her nails were bitten to the quick. She knew that it had been noted. Even tearing out her hair would make little impression on Mrs Holmes if she could not sob out her woes.

On Monday, when she had wanted to preserve as much dignity as was consistent with being apprehended for shop-lifting, she had vomited on the floor of the police interview room. Today, when she wanted to manifest the greatest possible feebleness and suffering, her complexion had its usual healthy glow and her voice was firm. She would just have to do her best.

Linda sat perfectly still in her armchair for several minutes after Mrs Holmes had left. She had played things in completely the wrong way. She had been jollied along with brisk reassurance. 'Probably no action will be taken at the Cloughton end. You'll have to go for the hearing in Birmingham, of course, but Dr Flint and I will speak up for you.

'It was wrong of you, of course, but it was only to be expected in your circumstances that you'd break down in some way. It was just a cry for help and we'll make sure that you get it. Even if there is something in the *Clarion*, it will be a nine-day wonder and then everybody will forget about it.'

The little eyes had twinkled at her out of rolls of flesh. She had watched the thick lips mouthing platitudes that she didn't want to hear. She had shut out the sound, unfocused her eyes so that she saw just a blur. The blur sharpened in her mind, became a picture of Georgina Groves, coolly nodding from the other side of the street without making any move towards her.

She had blinked and tuned in again to Mrs Holmes. 'And do stop worrying about Helena. You've taken the very best care of her for more than three years, given her everything she's needed. No one will dream of trying to take her away from you. And even if you were anxious to be rid of her, our resources are at full stretch and it would quite likely be impossible to find somewhere that could take her.'

With a hearty laugh, she had reached towards the tea-tray that Linda had, at the last minute, decided to provide, and taken the last biscuit. 'My goodness, if that's how you look when I bring you *good* news...'

Chapter Fifteen

By Thursday, canoeing night again, Zoe was feeling seriously at odds with life. This week, she had thought she would be able to enjoy her exercise without having to pay too big a price for it in the matter of protesting and aching muscles in her shoulders and upper arms. She had suffered this affliction cheerfully, reassured by a faint odour of liniment hanging around Frank on a few of the preceding Fridays that he too had been suffering from the unaccustomed exercise of certain of his muscles.

She was determined that she would obey doctor's orders implicitly so that her lay-off would be for one week only. She had been allowed up for a couple of hours today and had spent one of them preparing supper, which was keeping hot as she reached for the paper to skim the headlines. Frank came in as she reached page four. He draped an affectionate arm across her shoulders as he risked suggesting, 'Read it to me whilst I set the table.'

Zoe obliged. '"The councillor in our spotlight this week is perhaps the one that the man in the Cloughton street feels he knows better than any other..."'

'That won't go down too well with some of the others.'

'"....and yet, in our interview yesterday, he revealed facts about himself that were hitherto quite unsuspected. At first, as he predicted that I would be, I was shocked. However, before, our session was over, my respect for this untiring public servant was greater than before. He revealed details of a life spent beating his breast for a youthful indiscretion that a less upright man would have laughed off or forgotten.

'"Considering the nature of the revelations Mr Glasby had for us, he suggested that it would be a good idea to abandon our usual pattern of a short introduction followed by the stock questions that all our councillors answer.

'"However, the *Clarion* decided that the impact of what Mr Glasby wished to tell us with such sincere regret would be all the greater if it was conveyed in the familiar format."'

'I can't wait!' Frank rummaged in a drawer for cutlery as the questions followed.

'"TELL US ABOUT YOUR CHILDHOOD. It was very happy and rather privileged. My father sent me to a state school, of course, but we enjoyed many of the good things of life and travelled a good deal. Surprisingly, it wasn't all easy. I often felt guilty because I was so much more fortunate than my classmates and, occasionally, they showed me that they resented it.

WHAT ARE YOUR HOBBIES? I've never been very clever or sporty so my hobbies are important to me. I read newspapers and have always taken a great pride in having an up-to-date knowledge of world affairs. Also, I'm a keen fisherman.

WHAT IS YOUR EVERYDAY JOB? I work in the family firm. It's a small engineering plant, as I expect all your readers know, so I have to be able to turn my hand to anything. It's difficult to define my exact position.

HOW DID YOU FIRST COME TO EMBARK ON A LIFE OF PUBLIC SERVICE? Having once done someone a great disservice, which I'll explain later, I felt I had something to expiate. Also, I felt responsible to those less fortunate than myself. The people of Cloughton made things easy for me by voting me to a position where I could do some good."'

'I've finished the table,' Frank announced. Zoe tossed him the paper. 'You can read the rest to me while I dish up.' Frank settled himself in an armchair.

'"WHAT WAS YOUR MOST EM-BARRASSING MOMENT?"'

'He's capable of embarrassment? Skip that bit.'

'OK. "WHOM DO YOU MOST AD-MIRE? The Princess Royal. She sets herself the same task as me and performs it with greater effect, with more dedication and with immense dignity."'

'Well, I won't argue with that.'

'"HOW WOULD YOU LIKE TO BE REMEMBERED? As someone who tried to put back into life a few of the many blessings it showered on him."' Frank was unsure whether Zoe's exclamation of disgust was caused by Glasby's obsequiousness or the small gravy splash she had just made on the clean table-cloth. '"And as someone who managed to atone for his greatest mistake.

'"WHAT IS YOUR GREATEST RE-GRET? This is my moment of confession. When I was very young, too young to leave school, I fancied myself as one of the world's great lovers. I had my fair share of good looks and had made some easy conquests, so I decided to test my prowess on an older girl. The affair went

262

further than it should have done and the result was an abortion, which left the lady concerned ill and depressed. That is my deepest regret. I am comforted by her subsequent glittering career, and by her obvious enthusiasm for revisiting her home town to delight us with her music. Perhaps I am being conceited in feeling that anything that I, an ordinary humble citizen, might do could ruin such a sparkling life."

'What a creep! And what a shame to rake such a thing up again after all this time. Someone's sure to mention it to the girl. I suppose it must be Jeffie. Fair share of good looks, did he say? His hair's loose and stringy round his face in this photograph. He looks as though he's in drag.' He chuckled. 'Shall I go on to his opinion of his greatest achievement?' Frank looked up and noticed Zoe's stricken expression. 'What's the matter?'

'This article's my fault—the bit about Jeffie, anyway.'

Whether or not she was right, Frank could see that Zoe was serious. 'Can you tell me about it whilst we're eating? If I'm canoeing tonight, I'll have to leave in half an hour.'

Zoe transferred dishes from the oven to the table and their contents to two plates

263

as she recounted the veiled threats she had made on her visit to Leon Glasby to reveal the information Mary Lister had given her. 'I thought he might tell me what he knew to shut me up.'

She was not usually so naïve. Frank wondered what he could say that would be of any consolation to her. As they began to eat, the telephone rang. Frank half rose to answer it but Zoe waved him down again. 'You're in a hurry. I've got all night and the food will reheat.'

Frank tried to gauge her tone. Was she still worried about the piece in the newspaper and the effect it might have on Jeffie and Mary Lister, or was she upset because he was canoeing without her? He had spent most of his spare moments that day wondering whether to stay in with her tonight, bring in a video and suggest they spend the evening watching it together. In the end, he had decided that this would make her more angry than grateful. Had he got it wrong?

He speared the last two pieces of pork and carrot and regarded the sea of delicious sauce that remained on his plate. He had no intention of wasting it. He fetched a slice of bread from the kitchen, dropped it on to his plate and watched it absorb the reddish-brown liquid. He hoped his future mother-in-law would not choose this moment to call.

Zoe had not noticed. She had recognized Linda's voice immediately. 'I got your number out of the book. I'm only ringing you at home because I'm desperate. Please come here to see me, straight away.'

Zoe's reply was sharp. 'Have you rung Peter yet? He really is very worried about you...'

Linda was not listening. 'I can't come to you. Helena is asleep in bed. If you don't come, I'll do something...'

'But I can't get into your house. You know that. It's why you arranged to have the funeral in that very nice restaurant—'

But the click of the receiver being put down had already sounded. She looked helplessly at Frank.

He went on eating soggy bread. 'I can guess who that was. You're not going anywhere.'

She beat a quiet tattoo with her fingers on the arm of the wheelchair until she'd obtained his compromise.

'All right. Just for your benefit, when I've had some coffee and collected my gear, I'll call in on my way to the club. She's probably just enjoying a bit of melodrama, taking advantage of you.'

'She won't know I've spent the week incarcerated here.'

'Then I'll tell her. It's time she realized

she isn't the only one with troubles. If by any chance there's a genuine crisis, I'll stay with the child and let Linda drive over to you. Either way, I'll ring from there to let you know.'

Satisfied, Zoe made his coffee and twenty minutes later he set off across town.

Frank's attitude to Linda Crowther was ambivalent. Becoming involved in her affairs had given Zoe a new purpose. All her clients at Relate had given Zoe as much as she had given them, but Linda especially had given her a sense of being responsible. Zoe had been positive in every aspect of her recovery, but you couldn't be positive in a vacuum, and about nothing in particular. You had to have a short-term goal and sorting out Linda Crowther had become Zoe's.

It always surprised him when she managed to be so patient with self-pitying, introspective people. She had had scant sympathy with Anne-Marie's teenage histrionics, even after their father had been killed.

Frank drew up outside Linda's house. No lights were on. Was she round the back, or had she realized that Zoe was unable to get into her house and set off on the reverse of his own journey? Maybe the child had been left alone. He'd better climb out and do something.

The front garden was small, only just separating the house from the street. As soon as Frank opened the car door, he heard the throbbing of the engine in the garage. It took him ten seconds to reach the door and a further fifteen to master the faulty catch. In his mind it seemed like an hour, plenty of time for his calculations.

The journey had taken about ten minutes. Would Linda have allowed time for Zoe to abandon whatever she was doing and transfer herself and her chair to her car? And time to get out again to raise the alarm? There was no way Zoe could have raised this door herself.

Her phone call meant this was not a serious suicide attempt. Had his deliberately leisurely enjoyment of his coffee made it a successful one? At last the door was moving. He took a deep breath before plunging inside. Unsure about the effect of carbon monoxide on the eyes, he peered through slits and hauled open the driver's door, working by touch. His right hand turned the ignition key as his left grabbed the neck of Linda's jacket.

He tugged till he had the leverage he needed, then squatted low till he had slung her over his shoulder before carrying her in a fireman's lift out on to the tiny lawn. Her face was the bright cherry red he had been expecting and the veins in her neck were swollen and congested. He felt just a flutter of a pulse. Swiftly and efficiently he began artificial respiration.

A neighbour, come to investigate the commotion, was dispatched to ring for an ambulance. It arrived, with commendable speed and breathing apparatus. Frank was relieved when the neighbour, reluctant to have her hour of glory curtailed, proved anxious to be the one to accompany the patient to hospital. Parrying the questions of the crowd, mostly women, that had collected in the street, he turned back towards the house. 'If you want to be useful, one of you could perhaps take charge of the little girl until some other arrangement can be made?'

He found the front door unlocked and the child snoring peacefully. Returning to the front door, he found that the crowd had disappeared.

Frank had made his promised phone call to Zoe but had confined it to 'I'm coming back. I'll be with you as soon as I can.'

Zoe was suddenly sure that Linda had tried to kill herself. She enquired urgently of the mouthpiece, 'Is she dead?' but received only a high-pitched hum for a reply. That was the second time this evening that someone had hung up on her.

She settled to wait as patiently as she could. Washing up the supper dishes occupied a quarter of an hour. She thought about ringing Laura to confirm that she would put in a session at Relate the following afternoon but decided against it. Better to leave the line free.

Noticing the time, she realized that her two hours of sitting had more than expired and she wheeled herself through to the bedroom. She would lie on the bed but remain fully clothed. She might be required before the drama, whatever it proved to be, had played itself out.

Mary Lister waited impatiently for her copy of the *Clarion* to be delivered. She had learned since her accident to fill her days cheerfully, keeping her house spick and span, entertaining a host of friends, many of them disabled as she was. They tended, though, to confine their visits to the daytime.

It was understandable, of course. She didn't go out at night herself. It was when she felt most vulnerable. She picked up the newspaper almost before it had fallen on to the mat, and turned first to the lists of television programmes. There didn't seem to be much on tonight, though. Never mind, the paper itself often gave her much to reflect on—all of human nature, especially the aspects of it manifested in this highly individual town.

She turned over another page and found herself staring at a large portrait of Leon Glasby. What a mess of a man he was, mean mouth simpering, straggling hair, half in and half out of his collar. If men wanted to wear their hair long, then good luck to them, but why did they have to leave it in greasy rats' tails?

Well, she'd see what he had to say for himself. It had to be his turn one of these weeks, she supposed. She began on the first column. It was quite amusing that he considered himself handsome, and she had to allow him a little credit if he respected her own favourite, Princess Anne. Although, reading through that section again, she suspected that he had only mentioned her to suggest that he was in the same line of business himself.

As her eye travelled further down the double column, she realized that she had spoken aloud. 'Oh God, no!' What a strange and unfortunate coincidence that, twice in a week, the story had been raked up—once by her stupid self. There couldn't be a connection, could there? Surely that sensible lass had not taken it upon herself to interfere, to challenge him?

She dismissed the idea. Right or wrong, it wouldn't help her to know. The question was, would someone show the article to Jennifer? She worried about it as she prepared and ate her supper and decided in the end that she had better be the one to inform her great-niece of Leon Glasby's 'confession'. It would mean going out after dark for once, if she was to catch tonight's last collection from the pillar-box round the corner. She would use the hated telephone, too, to warn Jennifer of what awaited her in the post.

The girl's voice over the line sounded tired and cross. 'Thanks for the concern, Aunt Mary. Actually, you're the third person to ring about it. The other two merely wanted me to confirm that I was definitely the woman he was referring to before they passed on the juicy gossip. That wasn't how they put it, of course. It's good to get some genuine sympathy.'

Mary Lister scraped the remainder of her supper from her plate into the kitchen waste-bin. Curse Zoe Morgan! Curse Leon Glasby! And curse her own gossiping tongue!

Jennifer Lister smiled at her aunt's concern but did not share it. She was not sure what Leon was up to, but as far as she was concerned now, all publicity was good

271

publicity. She'd better burn the letter and cutting, though, when they arrived. She didn't want Laurent getting Gallic and emotional about it all. It would ruin his concert tomorrow night.

She thought that on a world scale he had a better voice than she did, but his performer's temperament left a lot to be desired. She could cut out the most devastating of catastrophes during a performance and concentrate exclusively on her interpretation of the current piece. Leon used his music to convey whatever emotion was swaying him at the time. Sometimes it enhanced his performance, sometimes not. She was grateful for her own ability to be dispassionate. It made life on the concert platform—life in general, too—much more convenient.

She returned to the preparation of her person for a late-night supper with Paul Masterman. He had been impressed with the *Queen of the Night* aria at the Festival Hall. She loved to show off her vocal agility with it, however much the forthright Miss Morgan might disapprove.

Zoe waited with decreasing patience. Frank's second call, not quite so brief as the first, told her that Helena was safely in the care of one grandmother and the other, Linda's mother, was at her bedside. Frank, being the one who had found her, had been asked to speak to the doctor who was attending her, and had been kept longer at the hospital to answer the questions of two police officers who had arrived there after visiting Linda's house.

Zoe had asked about Linda's condition. Frank, exhausted by a full day's work and a hectic evening and fresh from his consultation with Linda's physician, had informed her that recovery depended on length and depth of anoxia, that if she remained unconscious for any length of time necrosis of the basal nuclei might develop, and that they were hoping that hypostatic pneumonia would not supervene. Zoe supposed that he would explain it all when he arrived. It all sounded grim and she knew that the ever-courteous Frank would only have confused her with medical jargon because he was distressed by the emergency.

Zoe felt frustrated and angry. Linda was her client and she couldn't go to her. It was good of Frank to have taken the trouble to visit her, and of course he had had no choice but to deal with the emergency he had found, but she had had no right to oblige him to offer in the first place.

Deliberately, she unclenched and stretched her fingers. There was no point in compounding the problem by raising her own blood pressure. She switched on the television set and flipped through the channels. Rejecting an American cop thriller, loud with car sirens and gunshots, she lingered momentarily over earnest gardening advice. Soon, though, vistas of herbaceous borders were replaced by close-ups of the pests that attacked them. She wasn't in the mood for nature in the raw and pressed the button again.

A costume drama failed to interest her. The love scene was meant to be steamy, but she thought the steam would all have evaporated before all the stiff velveteen and corsets beneath it could be unhooked. The remaining channel offered a film that might have had possibilities but was set in a hospital and so put her off.

She had felt pity for Linda, but it had been laced with impatience that was becoming hard to suppress, and now she had let her down. What had been special about Linda, what had brought interest and excitement into Zoe's life in these last weeks, had been getting so very nearly back to the police work she had loved. What she had refused to face, fearing it to be an infatuation with Rob Cameron, had been the thrill he had brought her of getting back to the hunt. Linda was special, not because she had insurmountable difficulties but because she just might be guilty of murder.

In her subconscious mind, she had been toying with the idea of becoming some kind of paid investigator, a private eye—a lovely phrase which so exactly described what they did—but she realized tonight that it would never work. If she were earning something, she could afford to pay a sidekick to do the legwork, but the climax of every assignment would leave her as she was now, sitting at home, having dumped her responsibilities on someone else. She needed to get a move on, though, with whatever work she chose. She would be thirty in the spring.

Suddenly, she turned cold. How old had Linda been when Helena was conceived? She reached up for her harness and began the business of getting into her chair. She had never been able to think properly sitting still. Besides, Frank would be hungry and possibly cold when he came in. She'd heat some soup, warm some bread-rolls, get some cheese out of the fridge to bring it to room temperature and open a bottle. If she and Frank were married before Christmas, she could be pregnant before her birthday.

Having something to do had soothed her before Frank came in but none of her decisions was reversed. Seeing his face, grey with fatigue, she decided not to ask questions, but Frank wanted to talk. He described his arrival at Linda's house and his prompt action. 'It was fortunate she didn't notice that the small window at the back of the garage was open a crack, and the door was stuck not quite shut. It took me what seemed an age to force it open again. If I hadn't taken such an age to get over there, she'd probably not have been too bad.'

'She meant to be found before it was too late.'

'You think that too? Why do you think she did it then? What did she have to gain?'

Zoe was asking herself a different question. Why had she not dealt with Linda's appeal herself? Not physically, of course, but she could have alerted the police and the social services. It was partly because Linda had never before done anything decisive and was unlikely to now. In so many words, she had admitted that real distress was impossible for her to communicate, that she could complain only of fictional suffering in order to manipulate. Zoe was not to be manipulated and both Linda and Zoe had miscalculated.

Linda knew in theory that Zoe needed time to prepare for travel, that she could not leap into a car and drive away. She had never, though, mentally sat in the wheelchair in her place, had never taken trouble to see anything from anyone else's point of view. Now that the woman was *in extremis,* needing her help more than ever Zoe could find no sympathy for her.

She asked Frank, 'How does carbon monoxide affect you? Do you know about it?'

'A bit, and the doc told me more. She'd have developed a headache, felt dizzy, then got confused. Then, muscular weakness may have come on suddenly, due to hypoxia—'

'Oh, don't come out with all that gobbledy-gook again!'

'Sorry. She'd have become suddenly weak and unable to escape. She'd have collapsed and she'd soon have died.'

'But now she won't?'

'I'll translate what I said over the phone. Recovery will depend on the length of time that Linda's brain has been deprived of oxygen. If she lives, she may suffer from long-term confusion, disorientation and amnesia. The effects of a softening of the basal nuclei would be Parkinson's disease. That will become more likely the longer she stays unconscious.

'Then, there's the danger of pneumonia. The gas is eliminated fairly rapidly from the blood by breathing clean air, but if

277

her respiration is depressed because she's unconscious, that may not happen quickly enough.'

'So, she'll be better off if she dies?'

'Who can say that? But maybe her son will be.'

Suddenly reminded of Peter's situation, Zoe considered it. Two mentally damaged members of his family to feel responsible for and finals almost upon him. And how would he feel about wishing that lot on his nice girl-friend? From the little she had heard about Rachel, Zoe thought she might stay with Peter; compared with the inhibitions he would have about offering himself and his problems to her, her own difficulties with Frank seemed laughable.

Frank sat back and closed his eyes. 'Will that do? I'm shattered.' She nodded. 'What have you been doing all evening? I thought you'd be asleep in bed.'

'No you didn't. I've been deciding to take a leaf out of Ginny's book.'

He sat up again, interested. 'A degree, you mean? Good idea. You've got the brains for it. What in?'

That had not been what she meant, but why not? 'She's managing to combine getting qualified for the future with raising a family. Why shouldn't I? Is there time to get a wedding arranged before Christmas?'

Chapter Sixteen

The news of Linda's death on Friday evening interrupted the television news that Zoe and Frank were watching with scant attention. Frank killed the sound of the derogatory remarks of a member of the shadow cabinet on his opposite number in the government and watched the silent mouth spitting venom as Zoe thanked and commiserated with her informant.

Presently, she wheeled her chair back to his. 'That was Peter.'

'She died?'

Zoe nodded and they sat for some moments without speaking. Then she went to the kitchen to make instant coffee, which both of them drank and neither wanted.

'I don't think...' she spoke slowly, wondering if she were being fair; 'I don't think that she'd have learned to be happy if she'd lived to be a hundred. Without Graham and without Helena, she'd just have gone along with the next person who demanded something from her, and ended up in the same fog of resentment.

'I either did too much for her or not

enough. Her problem was bigger than I could cope with and I should have advised her to seek professional medical help right at the beginning.' She waited for Frank's denial and reassurance, determined not to show her impatience with it. She was shocked, almost indignant, when they were not forthcoming.

He regarded her speculatively. 'Yes, I think you probably should. Mind you, that's with hindsight. We'd all do things better if we knew at the beginning what we've learned by the end. If you hadn't given her confidence that you could help her, she might have looked for what she needed in the right place.'

'A psychiatric hospital, you mean?' She managed to keep her voice steady and her dismay out of it. This was the first serious reproof Frank had offered her since her accident. She had waited impatiently for it as a sign that he accepted her as an equal, a whole human being. She was surprised that it had aroused in her a mixture of insecurity, guilt and fury. She knew that he was aware of her confusion. There was no need to conceal her feelings but it was important to show him that she could resolve them. She bought time by offering him more coffee. He had struggled to finish the first, but he valiantly accepted.

After a minute or two, she came back

without the coffee-pot. 'I can either give up Relate counselling or remember what I've learned when dealing with future clients.'

'True.'

The silence was not companionable. Zoe broke it to remark, 'It's very reprehensible, but my chief regret is not that Peter and Helena are orphans or that Linda had rejected Helena so completely, but...well...'

'That now we've precious little chance of finding out whether or not Linda killed Graham?'

She nodded. 'What does that say about me as a caring Christian person?'

Frank smiled. 'It says you're more of a police officer than a social worker. You knew that anyway.'

Before she could think that through, a bright flickering light from the mute television screen attracted their attention, then absorbed them. A substantial house was being consumed by fire. The lower floor was obliterated by clouds of smoke and steam. Great tongues of scarlet flame leaped out of a row of first-floor windows. In the foreground, black silhouettes of firemen manipulated hoses and water-jets. The picture compelled them, held them immobile.

Suddenly the black and scarlet frenzy was replaced by a predominant soothing green. The viewers were being shown a photograph of the house as it had been. Released from the spell of danger and drama, Frank groped down the side of his chair. 'Where's the zapper?' He switched on the sound.

The clipped tones of the glamorous female newsreader revealed an almost gleeful pleasure in the disaster. '...Although so close to the centre of this fashionable Leeds suburb, Fairacre is still set in about half of its original acre, and screened by trees, so that the fire had taken a relentless hold before it was detected and the alarm given. A spokesman for the fire service has said that the house, which is a listed building, will probably have to be demolished.

'Someone's lost a fine home.' Frank regarded the impressive Georgian façade with some envy. 'What a wonderful place, and all that land!' He grinned at Zoe. 'We could keep horses and dogs and geese—all manner of livestock—on a place like that.'

Zoe sniffed. 'Only if you stayed at home to look after it.'

'But, with a property that size, I could run a business and still have more than enough living-space. What a pity it's so far out from the city centre.'

'Frank, it's just burnt to the ground! Whose was it, anyway?'

They had talked through the relevant information. Now, a tearful woman with a heavy foreign accent was assuring her interviewer that the charred body that had been found in a downstairs room would certainly prove to be that of her employer. Monsieur was spending a quiet few days learning a new opera role. He was very pleased because it was a French one, *La Damnation de Faust* by Hector Berlioz, his favourite composer. He had been so proud to have been chosen as Faust. Her face crumpled and she could not go on speaking.

Frank and Zoe exchanged dismayed glances, as Frank confirmed, 'He was telling me all about it in the bar the other night, whilst you and Jeffie were still busy on the rehash of her concert.'

The French housekeeper had disappeared and been replaced by Laurent Gilbert's dentist. Would he be able to identify his patient's remains without any doubt? Was he at liberty to say whether the police had approached him? Experts who had made a preliminary survey of the cooling remnants of the house had not ruled out an electrical fault as the cause of the tragedy. An 'art expert' was invited to estimate the value of several original paintings that had been destroyed.

Frank pressed the button, but he and Zoe

continued to stare at the opaque grey of the blank screen. Eventually, Frank broke the silence, to observe crossly, 'You've been up six hours. You should be in bed.' Zoe ignored him and presently he remarked, 'I'm really very sorry. I only met the chap twice but I really took to him—much more than I did to Jeffie. You were miles away. What were you thinking?'

'I was wondering if learning an opera part could be such an absorbing activity that it would prevent you smelling smoke. I know people get burnt in their beds, but this was eleven in the morning. Why didn't he get out?'

'Maybe he didn't get to bed till the early hours and hadn't got up. Or, perhaps, learning a big part is so exhausting that he fell asleep over it.'

'Wouldn't you have smoke alarms in a place like that?'

'I suppose so, and where was the housekeeper, the one on the newsreel? Shouldn't she have been in the kitchen? If he was busy working, he wouldn't be likely to want to break off and rustle up meat and two veg for himself.' He glared at Zoe, who was absent-mindedly fiddling with the controls of her chair, so that it moved alternately a few inches forward, then back, but managed to refrain from comment. If this was her substitute for the restless pacing with which she had used to accompany furious thinking, he would have to learn to control his irritation.

She asked, suddenly, 'Can we believe that so many deaths in a related group of people are just coincidence?'

'How are they related?'

'Well, their affairs are all tangled up together. Jeffie and Laurent were engaged, Jeffie had an affair with Leon, Laurent sent a ticket for Jeffie's concert to Graham. Graham was drowned, Linda has died and now Laurent's dead too. We've been assuming that Linda's death was a simulated suicide attempt to get attention and sympathy, but what if someone in the group wanted all three of them out of the way?'

'Who for instance? You're being silly, Zoe.' But his face and tone belied his words and, after a pause, he went on: 'All the wrong people are dead.'

Zoe nodded. 'Yes. I could understand Graham having killed Leon for revenge, though it would be a terrifically long time to have waited for it. Linda might even have killed Helena rather than devoting the next twenty years to doing everything for her. Instead, we've got Graham, Laurent and Linda dead. I suppose there's no chance—'

The doorbell interrupted her and she

went to let in Rob Cameron. She was not surprised to see him and knew he was disappointed by his reception. Yes, they had seen the television news and, yes, they had realized that Laurent Gilbert was Jeffie's fiancé. They had met him in London this week.

This last piece of information restored Cameron's usual brash cheerfulness. 'A lot of corpses strewn around all of a sudden. Are you prepared to ask some questions about this latest one?'

'What questions? And who am I supposed to ask?'

'You could see what Jeffie has to say for herself.'

Zoe was derisive. 'Brilliant idea! What do you suggest I say? "Sorry about your cancelled wedding and all that but come and play detectives with us. It'll cheer you up"?'

Frank added, more politely, 'Zoe doesn't really know her well. Jeffie's hardly like to want to cry on her shoulder, still less be cross-questioned.'

'We might try Mary Lister, though.' Cameron seemed determined not to let the investigation rest.

Frank was doubtful. 'I suppose it's not quite so crass as contacting Jeffie. What do you think?' When he turned to Zoe she was already dialling.

The two men listened to one half of the conversation. Mary Lister had evidently not seen the newsreel and Zoe described briefly what had happened, omitting the distressing details. 'Do you think Jeffie would appreciate a letter?' A long pause followed, then, 'Oh dear, then I'm sorry I rang... Is she up here, then?... No, there was no mention of her... That's strange. She may be with the police, of course. She might decide to come to you later?' After another long pause, Zoe made her farewells and put the receiver down.

'Did you wake her up or something?'

Zoe shook her head. 'Apparently the old lady has a phone phobia. I've had the impression before that she wasn't happy using it.'

Cameron paused before pouring the contents of the can Frank had handed him into a glass. 'What did she tell you?'

Zoe shrugged. 'That she hadn't known Laurent very well because he spent so much time abroad, though he was based in England. Jeffie rang her earlier this week. She was coming up to Leeds by train this afternoon after a morning costume-fitting. She was to stay up here with Laurent till Sunday evening and she'd promised to pop over to Cloughton to return the necklace.'

'So, what were you saying was strange?'

'That the television reporter didn't mention her as a house guest and that she hadn't contacted her aunt with the news herself. It's not really strange. I'm sure she'd rather be alone, but you have to be tactful. Of course, if she arrived right in the middle of all the drama, expecting to get in, she probably is with the police.'

'Unless,' Frank suggested darkly, 'her remains are somewhere among the ruins too and haven't been discoverd yet. I'd no idea he was so local.'

'North of Leeds is hardly local,' Cameron objected.

'Compared with central London it is. Where's her place?'

'She has a flat in Blackheath. So has he. I wonder why they didn't spend the weekend there and save all the travelling.'

'They probably wanted to get away from the hounding of the press and the telephone and so on.'

'Oh, come on, they're opera singers, not pop stars.'

'And I suppose there's less chance of us northern yobbos recognizing them than the London intelligentsia.'

'He must have money on a pop-star scale if he's got a flat in a swish London suburb *and* a mansion in Yorkshire.'

'He's got a place in Normandy as well, but then he's been on the scene for a good while. He's older than Jeffie.' Zoe turned to Frank. 'What did you and Laurent talk about in the restaurant bar last Saturday?'

Frank shrugged. 'All manner of things. How wonderful it was of Jeffie to accept his favours. Her talent. His new role and how keen he was on Berlioz. He told me the plot of the opera but he made it amusing and used terms I understand rather than trying to impress me with a load of musical jargon. I talked quite a bit myself.'

'What about?'

'The surgery and about why I wanted to be a vet. Then I explained how we came to have the concert tickets and what we were hoping to find by using them. I told him a bit about your accident. His curiosity wasn't vulgar but he did want to know what had happened. I said how glad I was that you'd met Linda and got your teeth into her problems. Told him you'd keep them there till you'd got it sorted out. He laughed, said he could well imagine it. Oh, and he was saying how difficult it was proving to find a date for the wedding and honeymoon when they both had such a pressing list of professional engagements. He said they were lucky, that there are lots of singers of about their standard. They'd had the breaks, though Jeffie more than deserved them.

'He described his feelings for her as only a Frenchman would express it. I didn't think she was worth it. She's a bit sharp and quirky and bony for me, and she struck me as being more in love with herself than with him.'

Cameron had finished his beer and was ready to float another theory. 'You don't think he'd become a nuisance to her?'

Zoe considered. 'He was quite a catch to be seen around with when they first met. He could introduce her to all the right musical people. I suppose she'd already used all those advantages. If that was all she wanted from him, she might have been finding him a bit tiresome...'

'And who is all his money willed to?'

Frank was becoming annoyed. 'This is getting completely silly. Laurent had the most tenuous connection with Cloughton and the Crowthers and we're weaving a fantastic story of wholesale slaughter.'

Zoe shook her head. 'There does seem to be something odd, Frank. Before Rob came, we were questioning Laurent's being in alone and not being aware of the fire.'

'I bet she was putting him off. You said she kept wriggling out when he wanted her to fix the day.'

Frank was using his quiet voice, which told Zoe he was seriously angry. 'Everything's a game to you, Rob. That wasn't what either he or I said at all. The man's had a tragic accident and all this talk is just ridiculous.'

There was an uneasy silence before Zoe suggested, 'Why don't we see what Benny can tell us—if he's in. I haven't been able to contact him all week, though Jerry Hunter said he'd get in touch. I don't want to hassle him. He's been more than generous with time and information.'

'So he should have been. He probably got his case reopened because of what we've ferreted out for him.'

Zoe cast a wary eye over Frank. 'If you'll shut up, Rob, I'll ring Ginny.' Virginia, friendly as always, was not helpful. Benny had gone off to London on business connected with the reopening of the Crowther case. 'He's keeping out of your way, Zoe. He's quite prepared to be up-front with you personally, but he daren't have this Cameron character crashing around making waves.'

Zoe shared as much of the message as she felt was expedient. 'I can't imagine what he's doing in London.'

Cameron was triumphant. 'So I'm right! He's one jump ahead of us and the lucky blighter has all the authority he needs to poke around and ask questions.' Zoe gritted her teeth. Now Cameron was beginning to get on her nerves too.

Chapter Seventeen

Saturday morning found Zoe feeling bereft of a useful purpose in life. Benny, two hundred miles away, was still on the job, while she was unable to help.

She had had no chance the previous evening to examine her own reaction to Linda's death. When Rob had eventually left them they had fallen into bed and Frank had slept immediately. Zoe had lain awake, asking herself whether any of their speculations had come anywhere near the truth about what had happened.

She thought back to the Jeffie she had known at school: clever, quiet, rather in the shadow of a flamboyant, sporty friend who had defended her. Zoe could remember no more than a vague impression of those august sixth-form personages with their prefects' badges and their serious careers ahead of them. In any case, that Jeffie was gone. She couldn't predict what Jeffie the rising operatic soprano would do now, even if she had known the schoolgirl version intimately.

What, then, remained of the old Jeffie? Her aunt said she had become confident, sure of where she was going. Was she really? Or was she using Laurent's reputation and social success in the same way as she'd used the hockey captain's all those years ago? Either way, why should she wish to be rid of her protector now? Of course she hadn't begun the fire! No one had. It would turn out to have been caused by a faulty plug or knocked-over paraffin stove. But who, Zoe wondered, would be picking up the Gilbert fortune?

She wriggled her shoulders in an attempt to get comfortable and wished she could get up and brew tea without clanking her harness and waking Frank. Would Jeffie have arrived at her aunt's house by now, or would she be driving through the night back to London? If Benny had gone there in order to speak to either of them, he would be feeling as frustrated as she did herself. Eventually, Zoe too slept.

Both of them were roused early by Frank's mobile phone. They shared a swift and silent breakfast before he left to tend a distressed cow at a farm up the valley. Neither of them had been tempted to revert to the discussion of the previous evening and when he had gone she went back to bed, refusing to begin her own day until the sky showed at least a few streaks of pink.

Thoughts of Linda Crowther had filled

her mind for almost a month. She couldn't say she felt that she had lost a friend, but there was a big hole where Linda had been. She wondered how Graham's mother was coping with Helena, and where Peter was and what he was thinking, and whether Rachel was with him.

She would never know now. She had been Linda's counsellor, not a police officer, not even a private investigator. It was no one's business any longer to keep her informed about the Crowther family's affairs. She was acutely disappointed. Could it just be because her idle curiosity was unsatisfied?

Rob's suggestions were ludicrous. She could see that now. No wonder Frank had been impatient with them. If anyone had meant to kill Laurent they had chosen a strange method. To set fire to his house and hope he would fail to notice or escape fell rather short of being a foolproof plan. But, would the forensic pathologist be able to tell if a badly burnt body had been injured or drugged? She realized that the harder she tried to quash her nebulous suspicions, the more determined they came back.

The noise of the post falling on the mat tempted her out of bed. Continual disappointment had never quenched her childish hope that the day's mail would produce something exciting. She made herself shower and dress, fill the kettle and switch it on before allowing herself to collect the letters. The top envelope, addressed in a large flowing hand, with many flourishes, was from Anne-Marie. Zoe remembered the poky, backward-sloping script of her schooldays and questioned whether handwriting as some people claimed, really gave clues to character. It seemed to Zoe more likely that it revealed a state of mind. She wondered if it could work in reverse. If you practised easy, flowing writing, could it change your outlook, make you confident and easy-mannered?

She put Anne-Marie's letter aside. Almost certainly, it contained an invitation to yet another social function that would be uncongenial to her. She opened two bills and consigned them to a folder to await her weekly 'business session'. The big, brightly coloured envelope was an invitation from a mail-order firm to avail herself of their colour catalogue. An enclosure congratulated her effusively on her good fortune in having already been chosen by their computer to enter the second round of their exciting prize draw. Zoe decided her life just now was proving quite exciting enough.

Finally, there was a smallish, pale green

envelope. Zoe had seen one like it before, addressed to Graham Crowther. She held it for a moment, as her mind raced, then she tore it open, and extracted the three neatly folded, closely typed sheets.

My dear Miss Morgan,

By the time this letter reaches you, I shall be dead. I am sorry to inflict on you an epistle of such great length, but it is my final apologia and my last indulgence. Its purpose is to protect my dearest Jennifer from even greater unhappiness than she will already be suffering, and to achieve that purpose I must present you with a moral dilemma.

Let me explain. Two years ago, I met Jennifer at a reception given at the Ritz for a much more famous singer than either of us. Finding the great man rather full of himself, and most of the other guests embarrassingly ingratiating, we escaped and spent the rest of the evening together—after we had taken our turns at performing our party pieces, of course.

I cannot explain to you the effect that she had on me that night, and on all succeeding occasions. I was completely *bouleversé*. The voice was magnificent, the *gamine* appearance bravely defiant amongst so much expensive glamour.

In one short week, I knew that I must have her for my wife. I think—no, I know—that she soon began to love me in return, and we very quickly became accepted in our circle as what the Americans call 'an item'.

But, whenever I tried to speak about our future together, she became withdrawn. She would urge me to live in the present and not let my happiness depend on what an uncertain future might hold. Many times, we came close to quarrelling.

In the end, she explained her reluctance to marry me. Because of an abortion carried out by an unqualified person, she had contracted an infection that made a hysterectomy necessary. She could bear me none of the children I had been stupidly and insensitively projecting. I never found a way to convince her that, compared to spending the rest of my life with her, all else was merely secondary.

Other girls would have been bitter, anxious to lay blame. Jennifer blamed only herself. She had used the unfortunate man, she said, for her own purposes and had reaped the reward she deserved. She refused absolutely to reveal his identity. I think she realized that, although I have lived in London for almost long enough to consider myself an Englishman, I retain the French attitude to the crime of passion. If I had known where to inflict punishment, I would have taken matters into my own hands.

In the world of music in which we live, each rising performer making and dropping friends judiciously to advance his career, my Jennifer never forgot her family and her roots. I much admired her for returning so often to Yorkshire, to sing for the people who had encouraged her early and sacrificed to give her her start.

When she asked me to give a recital to the Cloughton Philharmonic Society, I felt honoured. I little realized the dire consequences that would follow from this concert that I so much enjoyed giving. When it was over, I was offered supper by my kind hosts. However, I realized that their usual practice was to go to the pub along the road. I was more than willing to indulge my acquired taste for English bitter, and insisted on us all keeping to the accepted custom.

In this excellent hostelry, I had the good fortune to be entertained by the amusing anecdotes of your fiancé and the ill-fortune to meet Mr Graham Crowther. Initially, I found his conversation tedious and was looking round for a rescuer, but then he caught my attention by enquiring whether I had ever met Jennifer. Cautiously, I admitted that we were acquainted, had worked together.

Immediately, he embarked on a story of their *grand amour* some years before. He painted a noble picture of how they had loved and parted because he knew that marriage to him would have held her back in what without him would be a dazzling career. As though anything or anybody could have prevented the world from appreciating such a talent!

I began immediately making plans to punish this creature who had taken his pleasure and ruined Jennifer's idea of herself as a whole woman. I was surprised as well as angry. Although Jennifer had never said so, I had had the impression that the man had been younger than she was and in that respect a little less to blame for failing to control himself. But this man must have been thirty when he made her pregnant. He deserved to die.

I drove down to Cloughton on the Saturday night you are investigating and rang Crowther from a call-box. I suggested a drink, reminded him of our enjoyable conversation when we'd last met. I had sent him the concert ticket the week before, just in case I was seen in Cloughton by anyone who would recognize me. It would look less suspicious for me if I had made an arrangement with him for the following week, in anticipation of his still being alive.

It was Crowther who chose the canalside pub that the canoeists use. I never intended to get as far as actually entering the place. Then his domineering wife, who had obviously been listening in, made trouble about him leaving her alone. I said I would be very disappointed not to take this opportunity to renew our acquaintance and he suggested that we meet on the Sunday when he would be free. Broad daylight was not in my plan but I decided that very early morning would have to do and I told him that that was all the time I had available on Sunday.

I persuaded him to talk a lot about his canoeing exploits and I suggested he might initiate me on flat water. He was thrilled and rolled up bright and early. I'd pulled on the fishing gear I always carry in the car boot—I've always been a keen fisherman—and I now planned an 'accidental' drowning. It succeeded fairly well. I got my rod out to show him and stuck a fishing hook through his collar on a short length of line so I could hold him down with it.

When he was dead, there were no marks on him. I didn't leave him or his boat at the weir. They must have drifted over soon afterwards. I made off but not before I had been seen by a man and two youngsters bringing their canoeing gear over to where Crowther and I had been in the water. I went home well pleased with my efforts. I hoped that, for those few moments he was struggling under the water, he had experienced something like the terror that Jennifer did when she thought she was going to die from her infection.

Then, two days ago, Jennifer showed me the *Cloughton Clarion* article about Leon Glasby. I leave you to imagine my horror. As a Frenchman, I was easily able to live with the idea that I had avenged my fiancée's humiliation, degradation, mutilation. I knew I had to keep the vengeance a secret from her—English people don't see these things the same way and I had no wish to worry her with it all. But now I find I have murdered an innocent man, or, at least, a man guilty of nothing worse than the telling of tall stories in order to make himself seem more important and interesting. I cannot live with myself and I certainly cannot either deceive or abandon my beloved Jennifer. The only way forward now is that I should share the fate of my unfortunate victim.

You will probably have heard by now the details of my self-inflicted punishment in the media news. I wish I had the courage to suffer by fire as Crowther suffered by water but I know I am not so brave. I have already drunk a considerable amount of alcohol. As soon as I have woven my unsteady way to the pillar-box at the end of the lane to post this letter, I shall inject the cocktail of drugs I have acquired. (There are some advantages in becoming very rich.)

Before I became a singer, I was an apprentice electrician. I have carefully prepared an 'electrical fault' for the insurance company to find. For the rest, a box of matches will suffice. I am trusting that the season will make the smell of a garden bonfire unremarkable so that the fire in my house in its well-screened garden will have taken a sufficient hold before any well-meaning neighbour calls the emergency services.

You are an intelligent young woman and will by now, I think, no longer be wondering why I have burdened you with this sad story. There is no help for Jennifer's having to bear my loss, but it rests with you to spare her the pain of living with my dishonour. It seemed to me, and to your fiancé, that you would refuse to relinquish your investigation until you were satisfied that you had unearthed all the facts concerning Graham Crowther's death. I present you with them in the confident hope that you will destroy my letter and let things rest with the least possible damage done to all the people concerned.

Yours very sincerely,
Laurent Gilbert

The signature was an illegible flourish, maybe developed for the autograph books. Zoe put the refolded sheets back into their envelope and said a silent prayer of thanks. Graham's death had had nothing at all to do with Rob. She wondered, guiltily, whether she would have been so grateful if the letter had exonerated Frank, then smiled as she realized that in no circumstances would it have occurred to her to suspect him. Nor, if she was fair, had she any reason to suspect Rob of collaboration with Leon in his fairly small-time drug-dealing. His impatient sympathy with Graham was likely to be genuine and not just a means of keeping him quiet.

303

She thought now that his about-turn in his sporting career was ample evidence of his regret that he had ever entertained the idea of performance-enhancing drugs, or any other kind. She went to make tea with the water she had boiled as she tried to sort out her priorities. To whom, if to anyone at all, should she show the letter? And what, if anything, should she tell everyone else?

What to tell Frank was easy. It had to be the whole truth, but it must not be told in such a way as to pass to him the responsibility for the decision Laurent Gilbert had called on her to take. She willed the unfortunate cow to require a whole morning of his expensive ministrations whilst she worked out what to do.

She wondered why this solution to the mystery of Graham's death had not occurred to her—or to Benny. The contents of the letter had been a shock to her, but in a way, no surprise. She felt a great pity for Laurent, and to a lesser extent for Jeffie; but her prevailing feeling was impatience with Graham, whose childish boasting had been the immediate cause of the misunderstanding, and with Laurent, who saw the solution to his problem only in terms of how it affected him and his fiancée. How could he have not thought

304

of someone else having, unjustly, to bear the blame?

She could not allow Linda to go to her grave under suspicion of murder, nor could she leave Peter wondering whether his mother had been a killer or his father a suicide. Laurent was asking her to suppress evidence, against all the influence of her police training and all her instinct to tell the simple truth.

How could she balance the claims of all the people involved in this mess, or decide which should be protected from knowing exactly what had happened? She wondered if she had understood anything about any of them. Had Linda loved Graham at all? Would she have been relieved, or more distressed, to know what had happened to him and why? She had little idea whether Jeffie would utterly condemn what Laurent had done or whether she would draw some comfort from knowing the lengths to which he had been prepared to go on her behalf.

Gilbert had no right to ask her to play God, to present her with this dilemma. For a police officer there would be no dilemma. If she showed the letter to Benny, it would become simply a piece of evidence, solving the case and finally closing the file. Was there any reason why Laurent's appeal should carry more weight than Graham

Crowther's? She had never met Graham, but his death, by its very occurrence, appealed for an explanation. And yet, to explain it publicly would expose him to ridicule as a pathetic liar.

The suffering cow did oblige Zoe by requiring Frank's efforts for several hours, but they were not sufficient for her to reach a firm decision.

Leon Glasby had left his garage open on Friday evening to receive his visitor's car. Once it was safely parked, he released the door-catch and they went into the house together. The conversation was laconic.

'Your fishing-rod's gone.'

'Yes, I lent it to a nosy policeman.'

'I see. As one does. What's for supper?'

Glasby became more expansive over a subject dear to his heart. 'There's smoked mackerel with horseradish cream, already cooked and waiting in the microwave to be warmed up. Then there's chicken in sherry, and sunburst peach tart. I've slaved in the kitchen most of the time since you rang.'

'Liar! I bet you had it all delivered half an hour ago from the local deli.'

'You've never taken my cooking seriously.' His voice was peevish. 'If I'd had to earn my own living instead of accepting the sinecure that dear Daddy was offering me, I would probably have been a great chef.'

306

'It's a pity you didn't—have to earn your own living, I mean. Then you wouldn't have been such a slob. Can't you tidy yourself up a bit, Leo? I'm not used to scruffy dinner dates. Your hair hasn't been washed for days.'

He pouted. 'This is how I look for lounging around the house. I'll get spruced up if you'll come out with me. All this clandestine stuff is getting very boring.'

'No it isn't. It's what makes it all such fun, dodging the neighbours when I arrive and leave, half dreading a knock on the door.'

'Great fun for *you*. What do I get out of it?'

'You get me in your bed as often as I can manage it. Isn't that enough? I can't be known as your woman. It would frighten off all the other contenders and there's no way you can keep me in the style to which I've become accustomed.'

'You thought I was rich once.'

'You were, compared with your rivals. I've moved on since then. Be glad that I keep coming back to you for the amusement you offer...'

'I think I'd like to marry you now. It's my turn for some fun. It would be fun to flaunt you as my wife, flaunt our long-standing relationship that no one guessed at.'

'You've got nearer to that than I like. Any more little flights of journalism and I'll find another *pied à terre,* to quote my unlamented ex.' She sighed. 'I find French clichés about ten times as irritating as English ones. Anyway, what do you mean by marry me now? Now I'm going to get the money, you mean?'

He grinned. 'That as well, but I'd like to look after you, make an honest woman of you—all that jazz.'

She sniffed. 'You don't need to look after me. Fate looks after me: keeps you here for me to come back to; provided Laurent when I was unknown and broke; removed him when he was becoming too pressing. It removed Graham too. He was becoming a nuisance again. Apparently he revealed our little fling to Laurent after the concert he gave at the Vic, but not quite as it happened. He transferred it to his callow youth instead of after several years of marriage to his frigid wife. His story had me as a dewey-eyed innocent and the pair of us parting broken-hearted, laying all on the altar of music. Some days after he got back, Laurent told me he'd met my seducer. I wondered which one. I didn't expect it to be Graham.'

'What did you ever see in him?'

'You didn't know him in those days.

Physically he was quite attractive and he was *so* flattering.'

'Since Laurent has been removed, shouldn't you be sobbing in front of the cameras?'

'Not yet. No one knows I was coming up here except Aunt Mary. I shall tell her I'm too upset to face anyone yet, so I'm sneaking back to London to be alone for as long as possible. I'll be leaving before it's light in the morning.'

'Won't your taxi driver have recognized you?' She looked puzzled. 'Presumably you took a taxi from the station to Fairacre.'

She shook her head. 'Some people who got on the train at Sheffield were full of the news of the fire. When I heard about it, I washed off my make-up and tied my scarf over my hair. I rang a car-hire firm from City Station and had someone bring a car out to me. The name meant nothing to him. I shouldn't think many car-hire dealers are opera fans.'

'You must have found a Metro a bit of a come-down from a Merc.'

She shrugged. 'I thought it was what you might drive if you wore a headscarf. No, no more wine, I've to be up early. By the way, if you really did cook this food, perhaps you really could have been a great chef.'

At half-past one, when Frank had still not appeared for lunch, Zoe made herself cheese sandwiches. The doorbell rang when she had hardly begun on them. She brushed aside Mitchell's apology, both for the interruption of her meal and for bringing his children uninvited. His daughter was struggling to free herself from the pushchair's harness whilst his son was using the gate as a climbing-frame.

'Is Ginny having a bad day?'

He nodded. 'It's not the infant, though. It's the essay. It's due in tomorrow and she's only done half the reading for it.'

Having been lifted out of the pushchair, Caitlin reached out for the banana on Zoe's tray. 'Thank you, please may I?'

Mitchell grinned. 'She believes in hedging her bets.' Zoe handed over the banana and went in search of another for a hopeful Declan. Maybe she could offer to mind the two of them from time to time as Ginny's pregnancy advanced. Apart from its being useful to the Mitchells, it was time she had some first-hand knowledge of what kids were like and devised some ways of her own for dealing with them. Perhaps though, she'd better have just one at a time to begin with.

Mitchell handed her an envelope, written on on both sides. 'It's all right. It's been processed.' Zoe examined it. On one side was a Newcastle-under-Lyme postmark and the Crowthers' names and address, very likely in Peter's hand. On the other, in painstaking pencil script, was the proud boast, 'The friend who rang me last night is an internationally famous opera singer. We have arranged to meet for a session on the river and breakfast at the club. Should you feel any interest in our meeting, I'll tell you about it when you return this evening. G.'

Zoe looked up. 'It is his writing?'

Mitchell nodded with a shamefaced grin. 'Ginny told me you'd rung. I'm sorry I didn't tell you about it as soon as Jerry found it, but I couldn't do with Cameron blundering about and poking his ringlets into everything.'

'You're not really being fair to him. By coming to me with his suspicions, he kept you in close touch with what was going on. If he hadn't interfered, you might not have been on the ball when the uniformed men searched Linda's house and you wouldn't have found the note.'

'Perhaps not... The phrasing seems a bit formal for a casual note to his wife.'

Zoe accepted the change of subject. 'Yes, but it's what I'd expect. He never felt easy with her. He tried harder to impress her than his boss at the building society, and with less success.'

'Didn't he tell her that night who was ringing him?'

'Obviously not. She'd put the boot in on the evening meeting. He was probably having a sulk. He'd have expected to have an eternity left to boast about it afterwards, with all the club members who practise on Sundays to bear witness to their having had breakfast together. So, what now?'

Mitchell gestured his temporary frustration. 'I'm not sure about the actual next step. The whole investigation's been a bit of a damp squib and there's not much I can think of to do, without Linda or Gilbert. Why do you think she made up the pirouette story?'

'Maybe because she didn't believe him, and, once he was dead, she suddenly wanted to protect him from ridicule.'

'The old man says that he'll cover my back if I keep at it in my spare moments. I suppose that's safe, considering he never leaves me any. We both think it's too much of a coincidence that Gilbert is got rid of as soon as the note comes to light. We tossed a few balls in the air last night. He doesn't agree, but my theory is that Gilbert might have had some unsuspected reason for getting rid of Crowther. Maybe, once he'd managed it, he couldn't live with it and topped himself. If I can find some connection between them...'

There was a resounding crash from the kitchen and they suddenly realized that Caitlin was not with them. It gave Zoe great satisfaction that she had swivelled the chair and reached her before her father. As she rescued her from the heap of empty pans the infant had pulled on top of herself, she realized that a great burden had rolled from her shoulders.

She dumped the child on her father's lap. 'We'll have some coffee. I've got something to show you.' She brought in the green envelope on the tray with the cups and saucers.

Chapter Eighteen

Jennifer Lister negotiated the slip-road and eased herself on to the M1 in the Metro which she had hired, not on Friday but on Thursday afternoon, not in Leeds but in central London. Anonymous it might be but it was inadequate to contain its load of carefully wrapped paintings, the smaller ones in the boot and on the back seat, the two larger ones carefully wedged behind her own seat.

She was glad the art historian interviewed by the television reporter had been reasonably unspecific about them. She wasn't sure where she could safely keep them until the nine-day wonder of Laurent's demise had died down, nor who would advise her about disposing of them. She had felt impelled to rescue them, after administering the injection to Laurent and before setting fire to the house. It was distressing enough that the fire would destroy so much of her inheritance, though it would all be insured, she supposed.

It had worried her that Leon might have had reason to go out to his car and might notice the bundles, wrapped in two king-size duvets. Fortunately, she had managed to keep him well occupied and well primed with whisky. Together with whatever he had taken before she arrived, it had left him dead to the world when she slid out of bed and left.

Mentally she checked over yesterday afternoon's work. On the whole she was pleased with the letter, though she wondered if she'd overdone it, made it too long, been too anxious to explain too many things. She had had to account for the drugs that the forensic people might find in any remains of the body. It was lucky that Laurent had mentioned a problem with the electrics that he was going to have a look at this weekend. That was what had put the idea into her head.

She grinned as she remembered the tribute she had paid to herself for not being too proud to return to her roots. Not many people knew that Paul Masterman lived in Bradford and that he usually made the trip to Cloughton when she did. She had no qualms about the signature. She'd forged it to her own advantage more than once before. The typed address hadn't looked right on Laurent's green envelope but, *in extremis,* he would be excused that fall from good taste. The phrases of the letter were exactly typical of him. She had overheard him describe her *'gamine*

315

appearance, bravely defiant', and cringed.

It had become urgent to dispose of Laurent. He was becoming almost angry at her refusal to acknowledge that he could tolerate and forgive her sterility. She shuddered at the idea of cluttering up her life with messy, demanding children. If Leon's old witch hadn't made her hysterectomy necessary, she'd have made other permanent arrangements years ago.

Tempted by the thought of coffee, she headed for the approaching service station. She was sure she had covered her back fairly thoroughly. Besides, she liked living dangerously. She thought Yves was unlikely to mention to anyone that she had cancelled her costume-fitting for Friday morning. She cheerfully locked her borrowed car and abandoned the Corot, the Matisses and the early Picasso. Motorway services had been anathema to Laurent. If he was hungry or thirsty he had always left the motorway to find a suitable hotel. Jennifer had certainly become fond of good eating and drinking but, with her humble origins, coffee was coffee.

She sipped it and preened herself on her fluent improvisation to Leon about hearing the news of Laurent's death on the train. She giggled at the idea of herself in a headscarf. It was even funnier than slumming up the M1 in a Metro.

She would like to have come clean with Leon, explain to him how she'd got Graham off his back over the drug-trafficking. She'd nearly dropped him in it, not realizing that his fishing rod and Laurent's were the same brand. She remembered Graham's astonishment as she'd pulled at the hook in his collar. That was what had given her the edge over him as he'd breathed in the water, his disbelief and her surge of triumph at removing both the danger to Leon and the irritation Graham threatened to become again to herself. The cheek of him, turning up at her hotel room door on the strength of an invitation to breakfast with him that she'd had no intention of keeping. She'd have left him to trail the streets till it was light, if she hadn't been afraid he'd be seen, maybe brag to someone about their assignation. It had been worth the price of a room for him.

It had been a pity to attribute both deaths to fate. Leon would have enjoyed the joke and admired her single-mindedness, but she couldn't trust him any more. He'd mean to keep his mouth shut but there was increasing evidence in his behaviour of the effects of the various substances he had consoled himself with when she had left him and gone to London, and he wasn't always in control. She hoped for his sake that he'd been joking when he talked of his intention to marry her. Otherwise she'd have to arrange a serious overdose for him.

She drained her cup, reinserted herself amongst her pictures and continued on her way to London.

Art dealers were puzzled when, some weeks later, a small Corot appeared on the market. Since it was believed to have been part of a collection destroyed in a recent fire, they believed this available version to be a fake. However, it passed its tests for authenticity with flying colours in every sense.

Questions were asked, many of them by DC Benedict Mitchell. Assistance in sorting out the resulting confusion was given by a car-hire firm in Blackheath and a theatrical costumier called Yves. The subsequent conviction meant, sadly, that another fine voice was lost to the concert and opera platforms worldwide.

Mitchell's wife managed to convince him that this news would add nothing to the three weeks of post-nuptial bliss being enjoyed by Mrs and Mrs Frank Carr in Normandy. The DC contented himself with meeting them from the ferry.

The publishers hope that this book has given you enjoyable reading. Large Print Books are especially designed to be as easy to see and hold as possible. If you wish a complete list of our books, please ask at your local library or write directly to: Magna Print Books, Long Preston, North Yorkshire, BD23 4ND, England.

This Large Print Book for the Partially sighted, who cannot read normal print, is published under the auspices of

THE ULVERSCROFT FOUNDATION

THE ULVERSCROFT FOUNDATION

. . . we hope that you have enjoyed this Large Print Book. Please think for a moment about those people who have worse eyesight problems than you . . . and are unable to even read or enjoy Large Print, without great difficulty.

You can help them by sending a donation, large or small to:

**The Ulverscroft Foundation,
1, The Green, Bradgate Road,
Anstey, Leicestershire, LE7 7FU,
England.**
or request a copy of our brochure for more details.

The Foundation will use all your help to assist those people who are handicapped by various sight problems and need special attention.

Thank you very much for your help.